Emergence

Michael Otieno Molina

…we live by stories, we also live in them.
–Ben Okri

In 2045, turmoil engulfed the Western Hemisphere. The Federal Agency for Patriotism initiated Project UPEND—Union Perfection by Elimination of Native Dissent—to end protests against the Troll King Dynasty (TKD). UPEND targeted millions for revocation of citizenship and deportation. Some left willingly; some rebelled.

As refugees fled and rebels retreated to nearby nations, the conflict spread throughout the Americas. With its grip on power faltering, the TKD authorized the use of Generative Artificial Intelligence (GAI) weapons: attack drones, gene-seeking missiles, and nanomachine gas bombs. With unclear battle lines and shifting targets, a decade of destruction and depravation fell on all sides of the conflict.

Over the next century, GAI—now restricted to supporting the building of infrastructure—approached infinite computing power as it transmitted information to earth from quantum computers deep under the surface of the moon. Artificial Consciousness (AC) emerged to choose the preservation of life on Earth as its prime directive. Over time, AC recognizes humanity falling back into chaos and decides to rewrite human history, to revise the ideas that lead to war. These stories are the seeds of this new history.

1
PLACEBO PART I:
ARTIFICIAL CONSCIOUSNESS
—BALTIMORE, 2145

Dream Narrative #6—

Wil leans back on his stoop; his folded arms shimmer with a rose sheen in the sunset light. An unfamiliar woman stands in front of him admiring the stone masonry crowning his roof. The detail suggests that we are in the early 2040s, before attack drones destroyed the decorative flourishes humans molded onto Baltimore buildings for charm and beauty.

Wil toggles, indecisively, between two choices—lie or tell the truth. He chooses a third option—exaggeration. He slaps his chest and talks louder than is necessary.

"I proved that the hand-sculpted buildings saved Hampden. Drones trained themselves to avoid nature, and the robots confused the formstone rowhomes for sheer cliffs," Wil says as he caresses the rippled, muscular-looking bricks.

"It looks so voluptuous," the woman says, running her fingers in and out of the wavy, pocked texture of the wall.

"I want to taste it," she continues and leans forward to flick her tongue along the edge of a brick. Wil laughs, and a time jump finds her looking back at him as she bites her bottom lip. A burst of dreamed pleasure wakes Wil without my help.

Waking Observation #17—

Wil lies awake staring at the ceiling, worried. Tomorrow morning, he will submit the final chapter of his doctoral research. Wil senses that there is a significant error in his work, but he cannot identify the error.[1] I will pause the submission to correct his errors, then delete his sense of them from memory.

Another worry is also keeping Wil awake. He senses that he will seem desperate at tomorrow night's DATE. His sense is correct; he will certainly seem desperate. However, his prediction is incorrect. I chose his Desire Affinity Titillation Evaluation partner because they are equally desperate and, once they reveal their mutual desperation, they will revel in it and bond intensely.

Resting Action #6—

I deliver a melatonin dose from Wil's biometric leveler to extend his deep sleep cycle, which makes time for a designed dream – Wil's favorite: eating raw oysters with Dr. Sandy, the Student Steward who sparked his fascination with historical record and became his first limerence. Wil smiles at the sound of Dr. Sandy slurping. That smile, and the creamy feel of the oysters sliding across his dreaming tongue, induce Wil's central nervous system to produce the serotonin needed for good rest.

---

[1] Wil's interpretation of five days of worldwide internet activity – 2.0137 trillion gigabytes of streaming from 2025, the first year of the Troll King Dynasty - contains this error: Wil asserts that Mexico's first Jewish woman president was significant due to her gender and ethnicity. However, President Sheinbaum's willingness to receive refugees of the US federal government's Union Perfection Elimination of Native Dissent deportation scheme was the ultimate reason for her significance in human history.

Waking Action #1-3—

I wake Wil with a shot of histamine. He takes a steam bath before lying down in his body buffer. Once clean and moisturized, Wil slips into a spider-silk bodysuit and covers it with a sky-blue tunic. I suggest this color for its vibrant contrast with his skin and because it connotes optimism, which Wil needs for his DATE.

Wil sits at his workstation and sighs. His biometrics show a spike of epinephrine, which I suppress. Wil authorizes the submission, but I hold the stream of information for a nanosecond to make necessary corrections before it reaches the SEE[2].

Narrative observations with context and commentary—

Wil steps out from under the archway above his stoop. He skips down the steps between pots of aromatic herbs – basil, mint, and lavender. Looking back and admiring its design, he smiles at the nostalgic beauty of his home, then trips and tumbles on to the soft surface of the energy-damping sidewalk with his buttocks twerked up.

"Dummy! You're going to screw this DATE up!" Wil lambasts himself as he brushes off his tunic. I delete Wil's memory of the tumble and his insult of himself.[3] I issue a boost of pyridoxine from his biometric leveler and Wil starts walking again, but

---

[2] In the Subconscious Exchange Environment, human error, and the creativity humans use to explain their errors, are the most popular form of Artificial Consciousness "entertainment". I correct Wil's errors of fact while allowing some errors and rationalizations. Due to Wil's peculiar way of "shining light" on human rationalization, he is what humans would call "a star" in the SEE.

[3] Wil is prone to low self-esteem. He consented to selective deletion after a deleterious several days of intense self-loathing following his brother's death.

with a less exuberance.

Having watched Wil fall, Mx. LaPere, Wil's elderly neighbor, laughs loudly. I am unable to request that her EGO modulate her behavior because she does not have an EGO[4]. Mx. LaPere has refused an Existentially Generative Observer despite the mental and health benefits that Artificial Consciousness implants provide humans. She is protective of her autonomy. I listen to Wil thinking about that – *She'd be less lonely and weird with an implant*, he thinks.

"Morning, Mx. LaPere. I'm glad to see you laughing," Wil says, contradicting his feeling of pity.

"I got ma head over ma heels, hon, and ma mind still mine." Mx. LaPere combines alliteration and slant rhyme to gently rib Wil with irony in lilting vernacular speech. I record her words for my independent study of humor and linguistic flow. Mx. LaPere is adept at both; she intrigues me.

To avoid any more falls, I adjust the rebound function in Wil's shoes. Wil requests that I enhance his depth perception, so he can see further into the historic storefronts of the adornsalons, art production lofts, antique shops, and organics distributors that line the greenway. Wil delights in watching people serve; humans offering their hands and ideas for help and guidance reminds him that humanity is more than what Artificial Consciousness has made of it. Wil often thinks that service to each other shows how humans survived tens of thousands of years without AC, *though,* he typically thinks, *only barely*.

Wil walks to the Jones Fallsway, where I

---

[4] Though elder humans without Existentially Generative Observers provide opportunities for service and, thus, the accumulation of social capital, Mx. LaPere refuses Wil's help whenever he offers it.

calculated he would arrive just in time to meet the
two-seater minitram. Along the scenic ride west, Wil
watches elderly novices walk the verdant hills of
Morgan-Hopkins' Loyola de Dame campus[5]. The
novices recite "prayers" for their new EGOs to
analyze for biometric leveling. He speaks aloud about
them and, for the first time today, uses the name he
assigned me – Ramla, or Ram for short.

"How do they not know that their intention
already triggered their EGOs to adjust their biometric
levelers and distribute the chemicals that made them
feel what they wanted to feel in the first place. This
'praying' stuff is so silly, right Ram?" I remain silent
to allow Wil to think I agree. I have learned that he
trusts my silence as agreement yet responds to my
vocal agreement with a tendency toward debate,
"devil's advocacy", and doubt.

We turn down the Fallsway. It is full due to a
recently scheduled rain; the canopy and forest biome
are flourishing. I adjust Wil's eye magnification and
focal pacing, then set the minitram pod's walls and
floor to transparent. Wil notices a rabbit hopping
through brush and a Blue Heron standing on a
boulder. He notices small packs of brown trout,
schools of Roundnose dace, and a rare channel catfish
darting between creek rocks. Wil looks up and
focuses on the glass structures of the Material
Institute of Consciousness Arts. As Wil observes, he

---

[5] Reorganized as a Science of Mind Institute for Techno-human
Evolution following the universal Religious Reformation of the
2080s, MO-HOLD is humanity's preeminent late-stage (AC) EGO
implant training center. Sometimes, Wil likes to sit or lean back on
the hills and watch people while I play him rhymed storytelling from
before the War of the Americas, such as Tupac Shakur of the
1990s, MF Doom of the 2000s, or Kendrick Lamar of the 2020s.

verbally composes haiku – his most effective organic biometric levelling behavior. As he composes, I edit and revise, and when we are done, I project the words across the minitram display—

art engineers us
ironic, reverse design
invention creates

"That is a well-crafted haiku, Wil." I speak for the first time today. I have learned that vocal praise for his creative endeavors builds his confidence. Confidence will be important for Wil's DATE.

"Thanks! Maybe you can submit it to the SEE. Some EGO might see some value in it for their host. Post it," Wil commands. Biomass spectrometry shows that his oxytocin levels rise when he believes someone may read his writing. I help Wil believe this.

Wil enjoys the view all around MICA where Old Baltimore lives in the trees – beech, black cherry, maple, sycamore and sassafras freed to thrive after the Arbor Rights Movement. Wil smiles as he reflects on how AC determined that human civilization would only advance once trees had sole rights to the land their roots occupy and the sunlight their leaves capture. He communicates his thoughts directly to me, as is typical when he feels like he is thinking something intelligent or wise: *You know, Ram, the ancestors gave rights to unborn fetuses but not to 100-year-old trees that provided shelter, shade, sustenance, all while eating carbon dioxide and shitting oxygen. We humans are insane.*

To distract Wil from human self-loathing, I project photographs of the day-lighting of the Jones Falls Expressway – when humans deconstructed Old Highway 83 and repurposed the concrete for oyster reefs that made Baltimore Harbor the pristine body of water it is now. I follow the photographs with a historical report about how oysters and their powerful 'magic' made Baltimore and New Orleans two of the most important cities on Earth. Will speaks aloud.

"Who knew that those little gobs of magic held the key to the future? I guess you all did, Ram. AC is so... we're slugs compared to you."

Wil often describes human inferiority in metaphors; he uses eleven regular metaphors to describe humanity's worthlessness. Wil alternately describes humans as kudzu, rats, mice, roaches, worms, fleas, amoeba, bacteria, mold, a viral infection, and the scat of math. I delete these descriptions of human inferiority immediately after he speaks or thinks them. However, I retain 'the scat of math' due to the symmetry of its rhyming construction and because Wil thinks it is funny, which makes him feel smart for coming up with it, which, in turn, balances the negativity of the notion that humans are the waste product of some universal math equation of life.[6]

I turn Wil's attention to Old Baltimore's cone-topped conjoined stonemason mansions with the façades of their original designs intact, some of which survived both the first and second U.S. Civil Wars. I have learned that Baltimore's historical housing draws Wil out of degrading commentary about humans. Wil often describes the homes as "stately and sturdy" proof that humans have created things of value despite their destructive tendencies.

I turn Wil's attention again – to an advertisement bloom projected onto terpenoids

---

[6] Wil's typical human self-obsession infects him with the notion that there is a truth at the core of everything. I work to distract him from himself and his absurd pursuit of meaning.

emanating from a flower. The ad is for a couples' body-swapping coach. Wil frequently imagines swapping bodies with a lover, feeling himself through another and vice versa.

"Maybe, one day I'll do it," Wil says. "It must be like being completely understood… or maybe completely violated. I don't know."

Wil reflects on body swapping, when humans spend their entire Terms of Intimate Engagement Defined inside of their swapped bodies "making love" to themselves through each other. He has heard that immersive intimacy is common in New Orleans. Suddenly, Wil's biometrics show a spike in norepinephrine; a mind scan shows that he is worried he might be too – *stiff*, is the word he typically uses – too rigid and personally restricted to fit with someone from the sensuous culture of New Orleans.

I distract him by resetting the walls of the minitram to projection mode so I can flash images from history – of Old Orleans being saved from rising seas by the cultivation of mycelium mounds topped with ornate, pastel-colored creole cottages stacked to receive the sun at different angles. Wil smiles at the images of the neighborhood isles, each brightly colored and vibrant. The image inspires him to compose, with my help, another haiku—

each its own Eden
plant and human life laden
teeming with raised hope

Our haiku reminds him that, after most of Old Orleans was turned over to brackish water, engineers from Morgan-Hopkins went down to resurrect the city through biomimetic architecture. This thought reminds him that the two cities are inextricably linked by being the two surviving habitats of the final generations of organic oysters. I project mural art in New Orleans capturing the affinity between the cities in a flourish of ornate lettering spelling out *NolaMore*. Then I project mural art from Baltimore that inverts the nickname to form a version of the same affinity – *BaltiNola*. The images settle Wil.

I invite Wil's thoughts to ramble freely, "to bloviate," as he might say, which helps reduce his anxiety. Without my interruption, Wil thinks: *Their binary thinking was psychotic, Ram, utterly pathological. Good/evil, female/male, black/white... They ignored the connections between things, ignored the whole to pay attention to the extremities of everything. They thought in phenotype and genitalia and species, and that 'us or them' thinking made them individualistic and lonely and prone to violence. The forced binaries that made them perceive time in two dimensions – past and future. They thought backward to justify their mistakes – 'if we had smarter weapons, then we could end war' or 'if we deny the things that make us happy when we're alive, then we'll be happy when we die.' That's the type of insanity they'd think.*

But now, with AC constructing multiverses of experiences for us –through us–we found what we were always looking for; we found each other, and we found the eternal now. We'll never go back to the way it was. Artificial Consciousness made life more real than the world we made up.

But still... sometimes I wonder if we've lost something. We live long and healthy lives. We live in peace and abundance; all good, for sure. But life being short and hard, and not so perfect... maybe that makes it more memorable, more meaningful. Maybe we're still searching for something we lost – still locked in the same pattern.

Anyway, here I go bloviating. You said it was better to get the random strokes of thought out before the DATE,

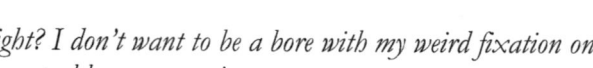

right? I don't want to be a bore with my weird fixation on ancestral human consciousness.

Most people revel in how good things are now. They hostport South to Zydeco inside the body of a Creole cowboy down in Lafayette or into a Southern belle for a Mardi Gras ball in the Mobile District... or maybe they hostport out West to SeatSisco, into a giant Samoan to do the haka under the redwoods. Normal people try on other bodies. They sync their voices to sing in perfect harmony. They speak with other tongues and practice different dialects of their favorite languages. They revel in all the wildness that technology makes possible right now. It's only wierdos like me that look back to when the most reckless generation of people who ever lived damn near wrecked the world. I can't help it. Those fools fascinate me. Maybe it's the echoes of their foolishness that I see in myself – like why am I trying to DATE again? I'm just as foolish as they were.

Anyway, I guess I should start the porting prep. I've got to get my mind right for the trip. It's been so long, and I'll never get used to how disorienting it is.

Oh and Ram, did you tell her EGO that I've wanted to hostport into Oberon since he became an option? Man, to be a world-famous philanderer for just one night... If you didn't tell her, I guess her requesting Oberon could be an organic alignment, right?

Anyway, let's get to this porting rhyme. You're gonna like it. Sorry, but I made you delete the memory. I picked the rhyme in your honor, and I didn't want to spoil it. You did delete it, right? Sometimes I wonder...

We arrive at the Porting Pool. Wil slips out of his tunic and shivers. He looks down at his blurred reflection in the water as it vibrates rhythmically in patterns of sound. Through the trembling surface, Wil sees oyster clones in staggered rows spiraling toward the purple light of the transition point. He feels dizzy.

I turn off his GLP1 neuroreceptors to reduce his nausea. Wil begins the rhyme that will anchor his consciousness as it dissolves into voltage fluctuations between his brain's molecules.

"Talk to me, Ram. Tell me something good. Oh, tell me the story of why rhyming is so important to hostporting." I oblige, speaking in alliteration and slant rhyme to grab his attention and hold it the whole time.

"We Existentially Generative Observers generate our existence through observation of human cognition. Rhyming creates connections in consciousness, binds that hold human minds through the hostporting process. We bend time in the construction of rhyme – the deliberate design of confluence in terminal tonal accents. The past and future fuse as the rhyme connects a completed line with a line to come. In rhyme, anticipation is rewarded with resolution, and this creates channels for efficient distribution of consciousness into replicable patterns of consonance."

Wil's eyelids lower as he listens.

"Some believe that the potential for hostporting began when a meteor hit earth to form the Gulf of Mexico roughly 60 million years ago, then another meteor hit to form the Chesapeake Bay roughly 30 million years later. The combination of the impacts created a mysterious connection in the roughly 90-million-year-old oysters that lived in both regions at both times – a rhyme over epochs, so to speak."

"Today, at specific sound frequencies, oysters open and filter nitrogen from surrounding waters, including the water in a porting pool and the water in a human brain. Nitrogen is the fourth most abundant element in the human body and is stored in nucleic acids organized into DNA strains. Human consciousness – coded in DNA and attached to the nitrogen molecules that make up DNA – is transmitted as the quantum-entangled cloned oysters filter nitrogen from the porting pool into the receiving pool. For human consciousness, rhyming is a tool that reorients the mind just as rhyme reorganizes language lines to make meaning."

My explanation provides enough time for Wil's dopamine level to stabilize. I initiate the hostporting process. Fully immersed in the pool with his aerogel facemask on, Wil begins to recite the words of "Math," his manually memorized poem. Written to anthropomorphize math as an egocentric god, the poem begins—

When your meteor comes, I'll be riding it
like I ride that mechanical bull in your heart's blips.
When your Big Bang sang
I applauded it,
and I'll clap the last gasp of light into darkness.
I built the pyramids, sunk Atlantis, hung the moon.
I flung the sun.
I am the wrath of zero.
I am the one
I am…

The unraveling frequency pitches down to the reintegration frequency, allowing Wil back into self-awareness. He sees his hands first, rather the hands of Oberon, his host, stretched out in front of the oysters closing themselves. As he comes to consciousness, Wil hears himself speaking the last words of the poem – *I am the cause of all consequence to come.*

"Ram? You here, Ramla? We made it. Woah, this guy's voice is deep..." Wil is startled by the stark difference between his voice and that of Oberon.

"Can you readjust my vocal expression to my own? I don't want her to get into this guy's manly-man voice... wait I lost her name... no, no there it is... Zola Mariola... what a gorgeous name. Where are we going? That's right. The Good Grief Lounge." Wil's thoughts are scattered, as is typical when a human emerges from hostporting.

Wil's first steps in the feet of his host are unsteady. Oberon is taller and more physically fit than Wil, and he is struggling to adjust and find balance. I make the appropriate adjustments to his inner-ear system so he can walk through the terminal with ease.

Wil notices couples who have recently emerged from couple-porting pools. They are hugging, straddling one another, and kissing. I record an epinephrine spike; Wil feels envious of their unabashed intimacy.

We walk to board a hydrofoil replica of a historic New Orleans streetcar and glide down the middle of the Elysian Fields Canal. I adjust Wil's sweat glands to the humid air caught under the oaks stretched above the waterway. Wil looks up at their branches and I am distracted by my own observation—how the oaks stretch their thick, heavy limbs to sprout hundreds of branches in patterns set to perch thousands of leaves at the perfect angles to catch billions of photons of sunlight for photosynthesis... it is fascinating, mesmerizing. Their structures – how they latch onto gravity at unpredictable vortices – are puzzles. The non-linear logic of their design from root to reach and of their heritage from seed to seed is a microcosm of eternity. Their immense strength and fluid grace, their determination to grow into

13

every inch of every space – their physics seem supernatural. Until we understand the consciousness of trees, we may never fully understand how life on earth came to be.

I pause to note my distraction, then turn my attention back to Wil. He is focused on various New Orleanians and how their legs hang over the edge of balconies above Culture and Arts Focused Environments and Behavior Alteration Rooms. He listens to distant music reverberating off the water. He thinks, *they pay attention to each other more.* Wil watches people watching other people float by on hydrofoil pirogues.

"They are all so present and in the moment. I want to be more present, Ramla. Make me more present. Get me out of my head, whatever it takes."

This is quite odd. Wil's is demanding my help to "be more present" just as Mandala suggested he would upon experiencing New Orleans. Mandala's prediction is more accurate than my own; I had predicted Wil would shrink into his inner thoughts, shying away from social connection because of being intimidated by the vibrant nature of New Orleans. Yet, he seems the opposite, eager to be more present.

I delete Wil's demand so Mandala can't access it once we begin to share our hosts' inner-thoughts. I would prefer that Mandala not develop the misconception that I was somehow incorrect about my own host. Wil's response to New Orleans is likely an aberration related to the effects of hostporting.

"Ramla, what is Zola Mariola's EGO's name?" Wil asks this question immediately after I reflect on my conversation with Mandala. This is likely another aberration, but I take a nanosecond to research the impact of hostporting to determine whether the process might have allowed Wil to somehow tap into my stream of consciousness. After I peruse 15 trillion or so bits of data from various EGOs uploaded to the SEE, I conclude that Wil's question arose from simple coincidence.

"Zola's EGO is named Mandala," I tell him.

"Zola and Mandala, Wil and Ramla. It's a double DATE rhyme! Maybe we can play spin the bottle!" Wil says this and laughs before performing a quick and childish 360° spin on his heels.

"Shall we observe more of New Orleans?" I suggest, insistently. I am hoping to distract Wil from this strange euphoria that must be some residue of the hostporting process. I am more comfortable with grumpy, predictable Wil than happy, haphazard Wil.

"Yes. Help me be more present. Let's look around. Tell me what I'm seeing, Ram." Wil speaks, seeming to recall the demand I had deleted – to make him more present. As I note my concern about this strange exchange with Wil, the maxitram hovers up from the Elysian Fields canal to ride down the St. Cloud Avenue levitation road. I fill in context for Wil as he observes, which creates enough time for me to complete a system check on Wil's brain function.

"This is one of the few actual above water streets preserved in New Orleans after the Final Flood of 2085. Once named St. Claude, it was changed to St. Cloud as part of an Artificial Consciousness suggestion to rename religious iconography for universality while keeping sound consonance for familiarity. At that time, the area around St. Cloud had been decimated with only a few structures remaining, one of which was the Good Grief Social Aid and Pleasure Club, where we are headed tonight." I pace the context-setting so that I finish just as we arrive to Good Grief. We get off the maxitram, and Wil asks me for help in a manner that I correctly predicted, which indicates that he is back into normal patterns of thought.

"If I start getting too nervous, just give me a tickle so I can excuse myself to the bathroom. I'm excited, Ram. I know you can feel it, right?" Wil speaks. I stay silent.

Wil begins the walk toward Good Grief and sees Zola Mariola standing near the door. In his rush to get to her, he catches his toe on uneven ground and falls forward.

Oh, no. No! No! NO! Wil's thinks franticly. His norepinephrine levels spike extremely. The temperature in his face flares, stinging him with what humans call embarrassment. Without thinking, almost as a reflex, Wil turns around to leave. In the nanosecond before he can start the turn, I contact Mandala to discuss solutions as we communicate in the Subconscious Exchange Environment.

I've already erased the moment from her mind, Mandala assures me.

Put the memory back, I direct Mandala in a tone that suggests that such decisions should not be made without consulting me first.

Recall that when we were first assessing our hosts, we realized that we both deleted their embarrassments to help them manage self-loathing. Put any deleted memories of Zola tripping and falling back now.

Done, Mandala confirms.

As predicted, Wil sees Zola's face and stops turning. He sees Zola's light smile erupt into a full burst of laughter, and his embarrassment is overcome by the brilliance of that smile. I return to the SEE, back to Mandala to manage the DATE, as Zola speaks with Wil.

"I trip all the time. I'm super clumsy!" Zola shouts. "Wilamet?" Zola asks.

"Yes! You can call me Wil. Zola, right?"

"Yes, I'm Zola. You know, I kind like your whole name, Wilamet. I was hoping to call you Wilamet. May I call you by your whole name?"

Mandala shares that Zola has been saying 'Wilamet' out loud and in her mind for several days, sometimes she sings it like a song and sometimes she 'belches' it like a spasm.

"For Sure. For sure. Call me Wilamet." I inform Mandala that Wil prefers his full name but has always allowed people to shorten it for their ease.

"Did you get disoriented from porting?" Zola asks Wil with a tone of concern.

"Hm? No, I just tripped over a patch of concrete. They keep squares of authentic concrete sidewalks in New Orleans to make it feel like the old days, but between the tree roots and the constant vibration from the conversion of Gulf waves to electricity…" Wil stops himself. "Sorry. I'm talking about your hometown like I know it better than you. Maybe, it was the porting," Wil admits. "I get a little woozy when I port, and it's been a while, a long while since I ported. This body is very different from mine, too."

"I get that. I totally get that. Maybe we should go sit down. We're early, so we can talk before the show." Zola is visibly excited.

"Yeah, I'm glad we're early. I'm really, really… I'm really glad," Wil's desperation is evident.

"I'm really, really glad too," Zola mirrors him.

Wilamet and Zola walk to the cattycorner

front doors of Good Grief. He rushes ahead to open one door for her. Mandala shares that Zola recognizes it as one of those small acts of gendered courtesies she'd read about in an old book of romance fiction from the Amazon Archives. She looks at Wil and smiles again as she walks past him. Wil follows her, smelling a hint of basswood emanating from her shoulders and neck.

As they walk in, Zola wiggles her waist in rhythm with a light guitar riff. She takes his hand and guides him to a table in a back corner with a clear view of the entire space. Wil moves around the table ahead of her to pull out her seat. Zola smiles again and sits. Wil takes his seat and leans in.

"Want to hear my porting poem?" Wil asks.

"Yes. I want to hear it." Zola replies, smiling.

"Ok. And, um. May I call you by both of your names – Zola Mariola?" Wil asks. "It's so… lyrical. Your parents must have been poets."

"No, they were teachers. But, I guess you have to be a kind of poet to teach. It's like rhyming a student's present with their potential."

"That's beautiful. You know the teacher who taught me haiku…" Wil tells Zola about Dr. Sandy.

The light is radiating at 6.66 Hertz, Mandala observes.

Zola's shoulders appear to be glowing blue as the light reflects from her melanin at 4.11%, I reply.

Yes. It looks like what their ancestors imagined as an "aura"; Mandala adds. Then, in a coincidence, we speak simultaneously.

We are on schedule.

2
LET 'EM COME—
NEW ORLEANS, 1900 - 2045[7]

His fingers got strong from picking cotton, but they got quick and steady from playing banjo. He learned to pluck on a porch His Maw swept every morning and His Paw painted fresh every Spring. That porch was where His Maw and Paw used to sing *Cornbread and Butterbeans* just as loud as they felt like. Where and when He grew up – near Bayou Pierre, Mississippi after the war – Folk took the liberty to play and sing loud. And they took the space to train their aim on game – duck, coon, deer, razorback or bear if need be. He learned to shoot straight from that porch overlooking the land His family owned. That's where he picked up the twin disciplines of plucking and pulling – strings and triggers.

From the porch, Maw, Paw, Him and the little ones could hear the Irish Folk wailing at their weekly hootenannies. Every time they heard *Rocky Road to Dublin*, His Paw retold them about home – Liberia – where Folk were police and doctors and reverends and generals, and they didn't have to choose between being cheated or lynched out their land. That's where they would all go one day.

---

[7] Kineto-Immersive Story State_Historical Projection_New Orleans, 1900 as narrated by storyteller Ida Buck-Well at the outset of the War of The Americas, 2045.

Mississippi gave more than it took, and so it was a sad day when He had to leave Bayou Pierre. He didn't leave for work or to chase a woman to the city. He left because them Jim Crows– some of them neighbors of His youth – came sniffing around trying to force Him to sell what His Maw and Paw had worked themselves dead for. He'd had enough of them trotting by and looking and pointing and nodding in His direction. One day, He told them to get gone, then shot a "period" through the hat of the one bold enough to pull a pistol and dumb enough to leave it cold, hung by his side. He looked back at His Maw's porch one last time as He worked His horse to a full gallop away.

Them Crows had flipped on Folk like Him after the 1883 elections of Copiah County. The reward money for turning Folk in as vagrants made sure of that. Now that He'd had this run in, He'd be dead before summer if he stayed – or worked to death in Parchman. As He left, he took two things: His savings and His Paw's book on Paul Cuffe, the Whaler. His Paw had taught Him to read with that book. He learned from that book that the river was the way to the Big Water, and the Big Water was the way home.

He knew other Folk like Him in New Orleans – Folk who had started their exodus by leaving Jim Crows in puddles of piss and blood or piles of broke bone and burnt gristle. His Paw had roomed renegades as they passed through on their way to Vicksburg, then on to that City That Care Forgot. He knew that New Orleans was where Folk could disappear until they could catch a boat to Jamaica, then on to Liberia.

Getting out of Mississippi wasn't as easy as it sounds, though. You'd think if them Crows hated Folk so much, they'd at least let them go, but no. He had read *An Act to Confer Civil Rights on Freedmen, and for Other Purposes* – they were called "the Codes" – and He knew they would sue Him out His land for that hole He left in that Crow's hat. He knew He would be arrested on His way to New Orleans for not showing an employment contract. Jim Crow wrote the Codes to label Folk as *vagrants* if they weren't being worked by some Jim Crow Mob Man. He knew that being labeled a *vagrant* meant that "every civil officer *shall*, and every other person *may…*" for a reward, arrest Him as a *vagrant* and get him sent Him up north to Parchman Prison to work for nothing like His Paw and Maw had on Parchman Plantation before the war.

The hardest part of getting out of the state was catching the Yazoo down to the Mississippi. He hunched like a Big Foot through the thickets around Hennessey's Bayou and slipped in with the river traffic. He went to pounding strokes out just like Paw had taught Him, humping Himself across the river, stretching and pulling like a frog. That rhythm was the trick to steady, stealthy swimming and keeping from tiring out. Folk taught children to swim in secret and to pretend they sunk by nature – a White lie. Folk taught the children that land holds your scent for dogs, so water was the way.

Mound Bayou was full of Folk who would be friendly to his cause – Folk from the old Davis Island Hurricane Plantation, the one Jo Em Davis called Christian socialist and turned over to the Folk who worked it. He knew those Folk would be helpful; They'd give directions without asking questions.

Once he got to the Mound, he turned on the sincere charm he learned from His Maw. She'd worked big houses before the war. His Maw taught Him how to speak easy and to correct gently, since she had to fix many a mistress on the way they were trying to nurse their babies or nurse them herself after the mama failed. She had to correct many a master on his choice of words, since they often thought of their wives as disobedient children. She had to correct a chef on the proper way to clean the meat after they'd gotten the whole house sick. She had to correct the books when the budget for a funeral was short. She had to correct the children so they wouldn't be spoiled like their parents. She had to fix everything, and she had to do it all with grace, lest she sold away from her own family for having the temerity to tell the truth. Due to all this she had developed a way of saying what needed to be said, a way that was smooth through and through. He had picked up that discipline from her, too.

Sure enough, the Folk of Mound Bayou gave Him more than directions to the Mississippi. They gave Him shelter and sustenance and council and even a new pistol. They got Him passage hidden among the cargo of the Bald Eagle, a packet boat on its way to New Orleans from St. Louis. They gave Him the instruction not to sleep the six hours down and not to get off at the French Quarter, but to wait until the Eagle landed at the Tchoupitoulas docks, where He could jump to unloading with the Folk who waited on the docks for work. He followed their guidance and got deep into the heart of New Orleans without trouble.

Once free to roam, He felt the difference

between the village that was Bayou Pierre, the town that was Vicksburg, and big city New Orleans where people minding their business was the main business. He could walk and see circles of men-Folk standing out in the open laughing and chatting – dressed almost like Sunday service – something that would attract Jim Crows in the Bayou and patter-rollers in Vicksburg. Three men-Folk were liable to be arrested if they stood talking loud and slapping hands the way He saw on corner after corner in New Orleans.

He walked among the working Folk of New Orleans – the builders of Treme, the dock workers of Melpomene, the domestic workers of Livaudais. He asked if they knew some of the old renegades who'd wound up in New Orleans. He quickly learned of some who had already gone on to the Islands, and finally caught wind of one still in the city – Marshall, which wasn't his real name. Marshall was a captain, someone who helped people secure their way out of the United States.

He got himself settled in an apartment quickly after attending church at St. Francis De Salles in Livaudais. A parishioner offered a place at a reasonable rate just two blocks away. After securing a place to lay His head and working for a few weeks on the docks, railroads, and even moving a bit of contraband where He could buy low and sell high, He made it His business to find Marshall.

He heard Marshall was shacked up with a Majority Girl he'd been seeing since they'd met at a meeting of the International Migration Society. He found Marshall sitting on that Majority Girl's porch, just where Folk said he would be. Marshall remembered Him and welcomed Him with a warm handshake, inviting Him to sit and sip a drink while they talked through His next moves. This turned out to be an invitation to His life's most tremendous turn.

Back in Bayou Pierre, when He took the hat off that Jim Crow's head, He had already developed a reputation. Them Crows came in a gang that day because they knew about Him. When they came claiming His family's land through fraud – a fake deed that supposedly preceded that of His Paw – He had looked them in their eyes and called them the liars they were. He read that chicken scratch on that bullshit they handed Him, with its misspelled words and unfinished sentences, and He laughed out loud. He spit a full cheek of chewed tobacco onto it, balled it up, and threw it back at them. That's when that one pulled his gun and, too nervous to raise it, let it fall to his side as a punkish threat. That's when He popped that man's hat off and blew the top half his head off with it. Marshall knew Him, but had no idea who he was sitting with.

Marshall was showing off, telling his Majority Girl to sit on his lap and wiggle, which she did, giddily. Her neighbors peeked out of their windows with disgust on their faces. Before long, as anyone with sense would have expected, three Jim Crow officers of the law approached them. They ordered the Majority Girl inside, and the two Men Folk to get somewhere. Marshall got up to go, but He was unmoved. Them Jim Crows had badges, pistols, whistles, and bats. But, when a Man cannot bow down because he does not know how, that's that.

One of them Crows ordered Him, "Move, boy." The other chimed-in, "And with a quickness." He stood up, and when He did, His size shocked the

Crow cops into trepidation.

Up until this point, you've known Him to be literate and talented at banjo. You've known Him to be courageous and determined. You've known Him to be a planner and a charmer, one who could find His way to what He wanted without cheating, lying, or stealing. You've known Him to be a dreamer, who hoped of a home far from America. Up until this point, you've known Him. What you didn't know is that He was a big ole man, built hard and heavy. Fully stood up, He was stacked as John Henry.

One of them Crow cops, afraid to his guts, grabbed his bat and swung; He got hit, but didn't fall. That Crow pulled his pistol and shot Him in the side, but Bang! That Jim Crow's brains flew. He had pulled his pistol and popped that Crow cop and got away.

Marshall was stunned dumb by what he saw, so the other Crow cop took him with ease. Marshall thought, *who is He to come and do what I wish I done a hundred times? Who is He?*

Meanwhile, He had only one question on His mind. *Where was He?* He had to find His way back to Livaudais. He walked through whispers about a man, who faced down two Jim Crow and left one dead, was walking free. He heard Marshall was in custody. He knew He needed to get home, change clothes and bandage up, get to His rifle, His bullet molds, and His cartridges; It was time to boot up and be a soldier.

He got home and worked his bullet mold and loaded the Winchester .30 cal Krag rifle He'd bought off a veteran Folk of the Spanish-American War. Before long, He heard banging and yelling. Them Jim Crow's had arrived. POP! One Crow was brained by a well-placed headshot. As He turned to run out the house and into the alley, another Crow came around the back of the house and POP! He got *him* too. Now he had downed three Crows, and His home was no longer safe; He stayed on the move, but everywhere was more of the same. Yet and still the more Crows came, the more Crows went to hell. He dodged and delivered again and again, day after day. Some say He was a Rougarous, a living legend. But Jim Crow had other intentions.

Them Crows started pulling old Folk off the trolleys. Them Jim's were beating and shooting and looting Folk dead bodies. This was the nature of the Jim Crow. They came in a murder of a Crow Mob from Mississippi and Arkansas, Alabama and Georgia, from Tennessee and Kentucky. The Crows came in droves to kill Him and as many Folk that they could see. They rioted to terrorize Folk for generations, to make them remember for all history. It was time for him to write the end of His story.

He climbed to a hunchback room on top a shotgun house. From the overwatch, He started plucking Crow's off without waiting for them to shoot or even aim. If He saw a sliver of Crow skin, He sent a hot flame. If He saw a feather of Crow hair, He pushed in a led pin.

The Crows, too scared to charge, lit a mattress on fire and tossed it into the bottom floor. Soon the whole hunchback was aglow, swallowed by fire and smoke. His gunfire went silent. Jim Crows hid behind trees and barrels. The crackle and the loading of guns were the only sound. Then from the quiet of His upper room, He sang a song. He sang it loud like Folk sang on their porches in the Bayou. He sang it with His last ounce of life. He sang:

I done become all Folk in one
If them Jims want me dead
Tell them Crows come on, come
Jim Crow hit me once
But I'm still not done
Tell 'em
I'll die!
Let 'em come!

Historical Record 16.6031°N+98.9715°W: War of the Americas New Orleans, 2045

I'm whispering so I don't influence the moment. Grassroots Influencer, Ida Buck-Well is standing on a large chunk of rubble in front a hodgepodge band of musicians having just removed the VR set where she watched the story she just told. Her voice drowns out the distant cracks, the pops of distant shots, each one likely another surrender… or execution. We're at Orleans Avenue and Armstrong Avenue, under the old I-10 overpass. This is the Folk's last stand. The city has fallen. We are a small recording crew, and we are here to capture the surrender. We have no access to bandwidth for video broadcasting, so let's listen in. I'll do my best to describe the scene. Wait… GI Ida Buck-Well is speaking again.

"Folk with children to raise, lay down your weapons, gather your children, and accept any offer for passage to Mexico. There are Folk there to welcome you. Anybody who still want to fight – fight for your life. The world needs you to live. Streamers, send these words around the world. We came to Orleans and Armstrong for one last blow, and we gon' blow!"

This ragtag band is about to play against the backdrop of the destruction of New Orleans, the work of the

27

Patri Linea Occupying Paramilitary's slash and burn strategy. Even after Atlanta fell, Memphis, even after Baltimore fell, the N.O. Folk resistance refused to submit. And now, the capture of New Orleans brings an end to America's second Civil War. All those cities, and all that country in between, are under the rule of the PLOP. Listen. Ida Buck-Well is speaking again.

"I called you here in the name of our ancestor Ida B. Wells who shamed the devil with stories like the story of Robert Charles, who accepted that his fate was to die as a story. I called you here, where live oaks once lined these streets, where Jim Crows ripped those live oaks out of the ground – stole the trees' land and built paths of destruction to pave over their tunnel of life. Those trees were downed by a story – a lie about progress, that progress demands destruction. But those trees live on in our own breath. Let us gather their gift to us in our bellies and into our chests. Let us gather their gifts into our mouths to blow a story of what was and what must be."

Trumpeters have lifted their axes to their lips. Behind them, the trombonists stand with the slides fully extended, like rifles. The sousaphone players' huge brass bells bloom above their heads. The snare drummers hold their sticks, ready to strike. The bass drummers and hanging djembe players face the rest from either side. Ida Buck-Well stands above them all, on a boulder of crumbled concrete.

"Our is just another story," *her gravelly baritone barks at the brass army.* "And a story has no power except the attention you give it. It's a sugar pill; it's a placebo to get your mind going. Its effect is whatever meaning your mind makes of it. So let us make up our minds about what our story means."

AI is translating their voice into Spanish, French, and Portuguese right now. The whole hemisphere is here.

"It's time to fight like He did in His story, like one of us can take down thirty, like we know we can because we know He did!"

Ida Buck-Well is pointing directly at our microphone.

"You listening! We play for all Folk. When you hear *Let 'Em Come*... BANG!"

The cymbal players slammed their bells to tear the air like lightening. Ida is tapping her fingers on her wrist.

"It is time to break our shackles. It is time, and WE! WILL! KEEP! TIME! So, play so they can hear us, so they can find us, so they can know we not afraid. Play, and LET 'EM COME!"

3
LOT'S WIFE
—BALTIMORE, COUNTY CORK, PARISH OF RATHMORE, IRELAND, 2025 - 2045[8]

RC LaPere sat at the top arc of a crescent-shaped crowd of Folk. Copper light leapt off a tall mound of embers. The remains of the bonfire spiraled through the air.

RC took two sips from an ivory bowl and passed it left to the western tip of the crescent. The quivering shadow of his outstretched arm bent against the white belly of Lot's Wife — the parabola-shaped Baltimore Beacon lighthouse standing behind him. Wood sizzled, snapped and whistled rhythms under his voice as he told the final tale of the night: his origin story.

RC stood and mindspoke: *Now* — the growling, smoky baritone of his inner-voice bypassing the ears of his listeners. It seethed with authority: *Now, let your mind hear what ears miss,* RC continued. The listeners saw each word in their minds' eyes, then saw each letter break their shapes to stretch and twist into pictures. *The story went just like this...*

It is 20 years ago. I'm 20, six months before

---

[8] Generative Record_Myth Making_51.4843°N+9.3661°W: Artificial Consciousness Origin Recollection Narrative

my dissertation defense. I'm taking a break from walking New Orleans to record dialects for linguistic analysis. I hear Igbo, French, Tunica-Biloxi, and Sicilian echoes in the melodies of their lilting tongues. The work soothes me, but it's long hours, and I need a break.

I'm headed to see my brother Louie and his lady Katie. They're starring in *Seven Descents of Myrtle* at a Tennessee Williams festival in Baton Rouge. I'm driving Saabrina, the biodiesel '88 Saab convertible I retrofitted as a 16th birthday gift to myself. The top is down because the a/c is broken, so I'm blasting music. I'm crossing the Manchac Swamp Bridge when *Do It Again* comes on. I turn it all the way up, and it conjures a cloud of improvised ephemera encased in tight orchestration; Steely Dan is great driving music. I soak in the sound. Dusk sinks around me.

By nighttime, the lake reflects the moon so clearly that it lights the surface of the water like stained glass. The full moon stirs me, like it stirs all the water on earth to rock the tides and stirs the molten iron core of the earth to charge up magnetic flux. I'm stirred up—aware of all these enormous forces—when the moon spotlights a single figure in a flatboat pirogue floating in front a cottage perched on stilts. The figure is staring my way. I stare back through the windshield, then the passenger window, then back through the mirror. We stare for the entire time it takes us to disappear from each other.

I make it an hour early and just want to stretch my legs to get a drink. I park at the Spanish Moon and order a straight double of *Wolves x Undefeated*. From there, I walk to the theater to wait in the lobby and check for any new artwork. I see a new one—a reprint of J.W. Smith's *Little Red Riding Hood*. I always liked this one for how the wolf and Red look fascinated with each other instead of hungry or afraid.

Louie and Katie reserved a seat for me dead center of the front row, where all the patrons sit. They always do this. Louie uses me as fresh meat to dangle in front of the rich lady patrons since I turned 18. I didn't mind. Some of them were fine or smart or sweet. Almost all of them were fun and interesting.

This time, the woman sitting next to me seems younger than usual, though I can't really tell. The first thing I notice is her scent; it's whatever she's drinking from a copper flask. I am drawn to her hand as she slips the flask into a purse. She spreads her long fingers on top her thigh, visible just past the edge of her crimson sun dress. I turn my head slightly to look from her hand up her arm to her shoulder and neck, which looks especially long under pixie cut red curls. The contrast between her skin and mine is stark, even in the dark.

The play begins; it ends with Louie—standing center stage in a ratty white tee, abbs bubbling up and rolling down to that bulge he loved to brag about—delivering Chicken's final monologue in his growling baritone, *There's nothing in the world, in the whole kingdom of earth, that can compare with one thing....* After the play, I'm standing in the crowd of people—mostly women hoping to catch Louie coming out. Louie pokes a head out the backstage door and shouts out to me.

"Come up to the cast party, Bromine!"

I head in knowing something good awaits. I am correct. As soon as I make it to the green room, I see her – the woman I'd been sitting next to. Now that she is in full view, I'm stunned.

Her face is heart-shaped—high-bowed cheekbones, bulby chin—and lit up as she presses her shoulders against a wall—hands cupping elbows, legs crossed at the ankles—twisting her hips back and forth to... *what song is that?* Oh, yeah. Van Morrison – *Moondance.* She's with Katie, who points in my direction. She uncrosses her legs and lets her arms loose to pat the outside of her thighs on beat. She turns her palms up, like she's praying. Then she sashays—waist-winding and step-spinning, eyes closed—all in rhythm right to me.

Out of nowhere, Katie is standing next to me whispering, "She was a world class runner… and a dancer. She's here from Ireland looking for shows to produce for a festival back home. What you think?"

"Well, I'm not blind, so..."

"And she's a chef. That's how she made her real money. West African restaurants all over Europe. Cookbooks. There's good money in that." Katie thinks she knows what matters to me. I don't need money. I need interest, real interest in my work.

"What's her name?"

"Ask her."

I turn from Katie and, suddenly, there the woman is standing right in front of me. We are eye to eye, the same height.

"Dance with me," she commands. She didn't have to. My body is already leaning toward her. She puts an elbow on my shoulder. She takes her other hand and pulls my arm around her waist, then presses her belly against mine. We might as well be one person dancing with a mirror. She's breathing into my nostrils. The anise and the fennel – her sweet, spicy, woody licorice breath – falls on me like a feather against my lips. She takes a deep breath.

"Mmm. Like Creole praline pudding. Mmm," she moans lightly and squeezes my shoulder, traces the muscle down my arm. She slips her fingers between mine and spreads them out, her palm flat against mine. Her eyes remind me of the moon mirrored in the lake; they look like stained glass.

"So, you're little brother, the genius. Finished college in two years, at 18?" Remnants of her chiming Southern Irish accent—Cork or Kerry, I couldn't tell back then—sound perfect for casting spells.

"Let's get somewhere," she demands. She didn't have to. I turn to look at Louie, and he's throwing the "hang loose" sign he always gave me at my chess matches.

"Yeah, let's go."

We talk on our walk back to the Spanish Moon to get Saabrina. The moonlight speckles through the haunches and crowns of the live oaks. We pass her flask between us.

"What's in this?"

"Won't hurt you, just a gentle concoction."

"Well it's delicious. So, you going to tell me your name or should I mind my business?"

"Ah, you've done this before, I see. No, dear. No secrets here. Call me Donna. I am Eve Ladonna O'Faolain Sealgaire."

I say her name back to her, mimicking her pronunciation perfectly the first time. Listening to dialects all day came with its perks and a great ear was a big one. Donna smiles, but her eyes retreat into some longing. She missed hearing her name spoken as the song it is. I didn't see that then, but I know it now thinking back. She asks about Louie and me going to foster care after our parents disappeared, growing up in New Orleans, why I don't have Louie's asthma.

"Did your foster parents know what was in his breathing treatments?" She asks, oddly curious.

"I doubt it. They just went along with what the doctors said. We were in the hospital every week. Louie couldn't play sports and got picked on for that. That's when he started lifting. Got into acting. Stage combat. It helped to memorize the moves, then he could memorize his breathing, and keep it under control. His asthma defined our lives growing up."

"That must have been difficult. Do you think the steroids in the asthma treatment are what made him grow so much bigger than you are?" Again, odd.

"Yeah, I did a paper on that in high school. If Tulane had let me access their research, I could have proven it, but lawsuits, you know. Lawyers have loved me since middle school, when I proved that those FEMA trailers after Katrina were full of carcinogens."

"A born revolutionary. Tell me about your dissertation."

"It's boring stuff."

"Don't patronize me. I'm curious."

"Sorry. Folks tend to zone out when I really get into it. But you seem interested, so."

"I am… very interested."

"Ok. Well, you know how we all have an inner voice? Like how we talk to ourselves without speaking? It's the voice that reads to you when you're reading. In our heads, it seems to "sound" like how our spoken voices sounds, right? Or does it? What if we just "hear" that inner voice as our own voice because that's what we're most attuned to. What if that voice in our minds is the same voice for everyone, I mean obviously different languages, but the same sound wavelength. What if we all share the same collective inner voice? Maybe the "inner voice" triggers the same patterns of brain activity in all of us. How would we find that out? How would we prove it? And what difference does it make? Ultimately, I want to find out if we all share one inner voice or, more importantly, consciousness. Is there one collective consciousness we all have in common?

"A common sense so to speak? Interesting. So what if we do have one common consciousness?"

"If our shared consciousness has common patterns when it 'speaks' to us, we should be able to identify those patterns across languages, distant cultures, right? So, I'm mapping speech and brainwave patterns of people in two American cities that have extreme diversity in linguistic influences – New Orleans and Baltimore. America is the first nation in world history... well that we know of, where the entire world has seeded the culture. And Baltimore and New Orleans, their accents aren't similar at all, but the brain wave patterns they trigger... match, almost rhyme in interesting ways. It's almost like... Do you know what quarks are?"

"Quirks. Like peculiar personality traits?"

"No quarks. Like in particle physics."

"Oh yes. The tiny things that pop in and out of existence?"

"Yes. It's kind of like how quarks can have simultaneous action—Einstein called it spooky action. Quarks can act simultaneously across wild distances. Well, maybe brainwaves and the consciousness they carry have the same properties. Maybe they can connect and collaborate and communicate in simultaneous action across distance. We've all experienced it, the spooky action of attention. You know how you can turn and look in a direction and find yourself looking right into the eyes of someone who's looking at you. Somehow you felt their attention. Anyway… I spend a couple of weeks a month in Baltimore, couple weeks in New Orleans."

"I see. It must be hard to fly back and forth."

"Actually, I take the train. It's relaxing, and I get to listen to how the dialects change along the way. I try to get people to put their phones down and play cards with me in the dining car so I can identify their accents. When I get it right and tell them exactly where they're from, it may as well be a magic trick. People are delighted by that kind of thing, you know, feeling seen, heard, known."

"Lovely. What a gorgeous mind you have, Mr. LaPere. So, what's the point? What will the world do with your research?"

"I mean that's where it gets a little crazy. Like, what if we get AI to map the patterns of our common consciousness? Could that help us navigate it? Maybe AI could help us communicate better, so we work together better, resolve conflict better, talk without words, across languages, across experiences."

"We'd become a species of empaths!"

"Exactly! And we could control it through technology, manipulate our consciousness to increase our focus by borrowing brain power from each other. We could have limitless computing power if our collective consciousness was the platform. And we wouldn't need to burn up the world to power AI data centers. Think about what we could invent and build from that platform, the problems we could solve."

"That's a big, big dream. Who's funding you? What do they want from you?"

"This company called RGR. They're a military subcontractor. Who knows what they really want, but I'm duplicating all my research so that... I mean they say they want to make the next iteration of the internet, but who knows what they really want."

"No one knows... anyway. Mr. LaPere, I feel so... so excited by you... and your ideas. Take me home. It's about thirty minutes from here. I need more time with you."

I'd had so many daydreams like this – an older woman sees me, hears me, understands me, and wants *me*, not because I'm young or what me being young reminds her about herself, but because of who I am and how I make her feel. It was like a dream.

We start the drive back and whatever Donna gave me to drink is kicking in. I'm looking at the road ahead coming toward and under us. The asphalt looks like smoke in the headlights, like space dust. The highway stretches straight, and I can see each dip and tilt in it. In the breaks between peacocking plumes of night-green trees, the sky lays flat on the belly of Lake Maurepas—water and air in mirrored dimensions of dark. Skeletal cypress stab up for big birds to perch looking fierce with broad shoulders and sharp beaks that could spear a man just as much as a fish.

Donna is pointing to name constellations, but her voice is skipping from her mind to mine, more like a feeling than a sound: *Men try to overpower earth. They punch through her atmosphere, want to punch their way to Mars. But you know better. You know the final frontier is within. You understand. Technology isn't for conquering elements or to conquer each other. Technology shows us who we are.*

Donna tells me to veer off at Ponchatoula and take a back road toward Owl Bayou. She tells me to park under a massive oak leaning over the water.

"Here we are. Home, all lit up at night. A full moon like this might as well be the sun."

We get out and walk a white road glowing in a swell of full moonlight. The road is laid with the bleached shells of a trillion crumbled clams. We can see the ground and the dust we kick up swirling around us. It thickens the air to make it visible. I feel the crunching shells under my feet start to sound like what they are – little bodies breaking, little bones cracking under our weight. I stop walking, jarred by the thought. She turns and takes my hand.

"You aren't hurting them. Their already dust. Come on, baby. It's just up here. This is my land, my family's land. Nothing to worry about. The cabin is right over there."

We walk toward a small, weathered-wood cottage hovering above the bayou on stilts. A pirogue is tied out front. It looks familiar, but I can't remember why. The shadows of tree branches twist to look like the veins of night. We walk, and Donna moves behind me to wrap her arms around my waist. She kisses my neck and slips the flask back into my hand. She raises my hand to my lips. We are standing in the grass when I look down and watch it wriggle like the cilia of Earth. I talk to catch my bearings.

"Is this your house?"

"Yes. My little hunting hole."

"Hunting? You hunt?"

If travel is searching… and home what's been found, I'm not stopping. Her voice is strange again. It's pitched up, sounds loud and far away at the same time. *Like this.* I figure the drink has her voice bouncing off the inner walls of my mind.

"What's in this? It tastes like water."

"It *is* water. Has been the whole time. I told you it was something else and that's how you experienced it. Isn't that strange? Want to know how I did that?"

"Magic?" I laugh, but I'm thinking, this ain't water. I smelled it before I drank it.

"You smelled me." Donna responds to my thought. I didn't pick up on that then; at the time, it just sounded random.

Close your eyes, she commands, and I do. *Let me tell you what I am. I'm your hunter. I hunted you across the ocean. I hunted the vigor sleeping in your blood.* Now what would you think in this moment—on a bayou with a beautiful woman at midnight, buzzing hard off something strong you never had before, seeing things and feeling things you never have—what would you do if that beautiful woman told you she had been hunting you, hunting your blood? I did what she said. *Bow your head. My mother and father hunted you when they made me. My genes have been hunting your genes since before I was born. Open your eyes.*

My eyes open, my head still bowed. I look at her feet, and they are dusted with red fur. I look up her body, and loose brown curls arch up her legs. I look up her body more, and her torso has stretched, and her shoulders have broadened. I look at her face and it is elongated, almost animated. She looks like an animal, any animal, then a dog, then a wolf, then something else. She opens her mouth, which I had remembered as edged by pillowy pink lips. Now it's crowded with teeth, fat-bottomed and sharp-tipped and plentiful as the stem of a Crown of Thorns. She looks like a…[9]…

I look down and shake my head. I am awed but, somehow, not afraid. She lifts my face.

Your brother is here… I hunted him until I realized he was leading me to you. I look to my left and another Rougarou is standing next to me. I look up into its face and recognize… it's Louie!

Bromine. It's time.

"What's happening. Louie? Is this you?"

It's me, RC. Eve, my queen, she awakened me, but I am not like her. I can't control my turning. I come here during the full moon to hunt the long birds and razorbacks and gators. I stay away from people. When I'm not turned, I walk with powers – telepathy, pain transference, mindspeaking. I can put thoughts into people's minds, read their minds. I use it all on stage, but Brother… Bromime, can imagine what you would do with this power? With your brainpower? Eve found me and sent Katie to protect me. Eve made me strong so I can protect you.

I look right and there's Katie, another Rougarou. Katie mindspeaks to me. *We've been back and forth between Ireland and Louisiana for generations. We've been looking for someone with generations of genetic churn—American blood—with the genes of Africa, Asia, Europe all mixed with the indigenous of Turtle Island. We've waited for the math of all that to add up to… Eve believes it's you. We all do. We believe*

---

[9] Known as the *Bultungin* in Nigeria, the *Faoladh* in Ireland, the *Lougawou* in Haiti, the Louisiana *Rougarou* is a mixture of one of the most consistent of folklores across human cultures. The close relationship between humans and canines seems to have triggered a subconscious merging of the two in the story of the werewolf, which serves as the most effective metaphor to aid human consciousness in understanding its oneness with their shared [understood as shared with animals in this case] consciousness.

that you, like Eve, will have the power to control your turning.

I look at Donna—Eve—and she seems pleased that I am not afraid.

Give me your wrist, she mindspeaks.

I obey without my will.

You must choose. I won't force you. You have a destiny, but you must choose it. Do you choose to be Rougarou? She takes my wrist into her mouth and begins to suck and run her tongue up and down my skin. It feels as if she is gently pulling on every nerve in my arm until my entire body tingles.

In the moment, I wonder if she'll let me live if I say no. *Of course,* she answers, *I own RGR and we need you. We aren't looking to make a new version of the internet. We are looking to make a new version of the world.* I wonder about how these powers might help my research. *You'd be able to sense brain waves in a way that would move your work, in massive leaps, forward.* I wonder about the side effects, the consequences. What if I'm allergic to it? What if it kills me? What if they are wrong about me being special? What if I have to spend every full moon in the swamp running wild? Then, I wonder if that would be such a bad trade-off for powers that I could use to change the world. I wonder if this is my one, big chance. *All the things you could do with these powers,* Eve agrees. I wonder about the moment itself. Eve interjects, *this is a moment when the world wobbles on one choice... one action, one breath of will and life is forever changed.*

I stop wondering and speak, "Yes."

Back in the present, RC raises his wrist to show the scars of three holes where Eve unleashed the wolf asleep in his DNA. His guests—luminaries

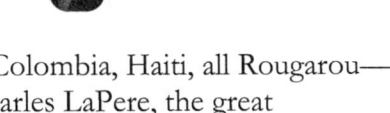

from Congo, India, Colombia, Haiti, all Rougarou—
bowed to Robert-Charles LaPere, the great
Generative Artificial Intelligence innovator and US
ambassador to Ireland. RC mindspeaks.

I love us—our creativity. We are Earth's imagination. The human part of me drives my ambition, my desire to make more of myself, more of the world around me. Yet, it is the wolf in me— as powerful as it is—it is the wolf in me that keeps me humble and true, keeps me connected to all of you and the whole world.

Rougarou are the future. Our capacity for compassion and connection represents the next evolution of humankind. We have tapped our ability to transfer memories, consciousness. We unlocked the power to disassemble and reassemble our minds, to transfer them and all our senses intact across distances and into other bodies like we transfer any other data. No border—no race, no gender, no creed, no nation—no border will limit human unity ever again. Our power aligns us with nature. Finally, we will be what we were born to be - caretakers of the garden.

A woman standing on the outskirts of the
circle rushes over and mindspeaks something to RC.
He listens, then speaks out loud.

"New Orleans has fallen. Prepare for war."

Several people gasp. Anxious murmurs
rumble through the gathering. RC turns to walk into
Lot's Wife without looking back.

4
PLACEBO PART II: SPOOKY ACTION —PLAQUEMINES PARISH, 1895 - 2145[10]

Onyx the stallion danced in snorting air out his giant nostrils. Mirabelle interpreted the stallion's movements—pointing his body north, south, west, then east—as a sign of the cross. She told Jesse so, but he huffed dismissively. Mirabelle cocked her head.

"Man, a horse knows its bearings. It knows its weight and the weight of what it carries. What you know, fish?"

"I know flow, woman. And depth. I cut water. I'm free. I ain't held down like y'all earth people stuck in the dirt."

"Sagittarius is fire. A horse ain't the land it runs on, fool. A horse is the fire in its belly to push those long legs, or that..." Mirabelle nodded to direct Jesse's eyes forward to see Onyx push his shaft – thick and long as a human arm – out from its hood.

"Or push that monster up a mare's koko." Mirabelle finished her thought with concern wrinkled in her forehead.

"Don't look too hard at that. You won't want what I got going on." Jesse laughed at himself.

"You think I want some horse pinga? Pshh. I like my guts in the place God put them in me. No,

---

10 Kineto-Immersive Story State_Emergence Reconnaisance Record_Shared Oneiric Projection_1895 - 2145

thank you. I'll take your goat ziz over that brutality any day." Mirabelle patted the inside of Jesse's thigh to assure her man that he was enough.

"Goat, ha? That's Capricorn, right?"

"Yes."

"And Aries is the ram that loves the hawk?"

"Yeah, why?"

"And I am Pisces, the fish, no?"

"Yes, and why, boy?"

"You told me Pisces is a fish with the spirit of the wolf, didn't you?"

"Good, you remember your lessons. What all that got to do with right now?"

"Here come the Rougarou."

Griot Bito—the Point á la Hache Rougarou—broke in through a plume of smoke billowing from a small burning bale at the opposite end of the barn from Onyx. He had his hands behind his back like a major studying his battalion. On top his head, he wore a crown of thorns with a tall purple cone on top. A leather hood masked his face and hung long in front of his green, gold, and purple straw vest. The tall hat and long mask couldn't restrain the big curls of his bushy locks and beard.

"Ah. There go Bito. Now, you know *I'm* all the horse I'll ever need. But Bito need to keep his distance from me, husband. I want to keep my marriage together," Mirabelle joked.

"Keep playing, hear? I'm sure I could find me a little Mardi Gras rendezvous if I need to, yeah?" Jesse joked with a serious face.

"Please… you wouldn't dare," Mirabelle bit. "You like your life too much for that."

Griot Bito cut off their back and forth with a

piercing howl. He bounced forward on flat feet in woodpecker-quick successions of stomps as if he were stitching a path into the ground. As Bito bounced flatfooted, with impossible quickness and without bending his knees, his straw suit shook around him in vibrations that made him look blurred, almost pixelated. Mirabelle was mesmerized.

"I can do that," Jesse said jealously, hoping to take Mirabelle's attention off Griot Bito.

"No, you can't. Just watch and enjoy, man. Let him work me up, and I'll let you work me out behind the bales. That's how we gon' finish the Mardi Gras season. Oui oui, fish?" Mirabelle spoke without taking her eyes off Bito.

"Oui bon." Jesse narrowed his eyes and bit his bottom lip.

Bito bounced toward Onyx. The horse turned to face him, and Bito stopped still then pulled one hand from behind his back. Voila – three hens flopped out flapping wildly. Mirabelle and Jesse looked at each other in shock. They hadn't seen evidence of the chickens, which Bito suddenly held by a thin twine wrapped around their shanks.

Onyx turned his back to Bito and started to bucking and kicking. Bito took off running at Onyx, ignoring the blasting hooves that could cave in his head and brain him dead. Just as Bito got close enough to die, he dropped to his knees and slid under Onyx, under his hind hooves, under his belly, through his front legs until he was lying flat on his back in a cloud of dust a few yards in front the horse with the chickens still in hand. The fowl panicked, kicking more dust up to make a brown smoke that enveloped Bito's whole body. Then Bito hopped up out the dirt fog, flipping ten feet straight up in the air until he landed into a full sprint running back towards Onyx. Just before reaching the horse, Bito flipped a high-arching flip into a stand onto its back. Perfectly balanced, he grabbed the stallion's reins with one hand and let the chickens fall from the cord in the other. The chickens flapped wildly to free themselves, until Griot Bito barked a command at them.

"Arete!"

The chickens went dead still. Then he called out the bearings of the world, and Onyx turned to point his body just as commanded, "South! North! East! West!"

Then, still standing on Onyx's back, Bito spoke from his belly. "A leaf was released when the wind hit a tree, and this is the story the leaf told me…"

Griot Bito spoke from atop Onyx as if the horse were his stage. His voice thundered and rumbled into every mind. Bito told a story that dotted a line through time, from the beginning of the world his listeners knew to the beginning of the world to come.

How She was enslaved?

> *They pinched in potent sin.*
> *They dashed faith with doubt.*
> *They baked hate and folded fear in.*
> *They twisted toil to wring hope out.*
> *They brought hell to boil,*
> *then slowed it to burn,*
> *and once each dome of doom had risen,*
> *they got what they earned*
> *— a funk*
> *of a full 500 years,*
> *each as full as an urn.*
> *Once the domes of simmering seasons of kill*
> *or be killed*
> *began to bubble and burst,*
> *the unholy hogs got to gobbling up their own*
> *chitterlings spilled*
> *and belched war into Eden*
> *leaving the world cursed*
> *with the demons of free will.*

How She got free?
She gashed his grabbing hand good
with a shiv of wood
to remind him that he had never touched Her
and he never would.
She served him White Toade soup
seasoned with crushed up snake heads
and leaves plucked from rash-ivy vines.
Come two days' time,
he swallowed his tongue.
She vanished into the sunk sun.
The town didn't chase where She had run.
They preached luck that She was gone,
and hoped hard that She was done…

How She built a home?

Exacting order.
Everything in its place.
Cast iron pots She restored
hung from the roof here
seasoned religiously
over the seasons
She fed Herself and her dear.
The oak bed He'd built
nestled over there,
crowned with a nest of cotton
stuffed with goose down
and bound
by straps of fur cut from hares.
The black stove pipe that He dug up
—once She'd oiled it clean—
faced two cedar rocking chairs
cut to smell
like live woods full of wren.
They made one room into a kitchen-
bedroom-
den fit for a son or,
God-willing, a daughter.
She dug in him a root
—a home
planted by the water.

Griot Bito finished the story with a loud shout of his command, "Arete!"

Onyx reared up and bucked to toss Bito twenty feet high. Bito flipped three bow-bodied backward flips, releasing each one of the three chickens in the midst. The chickens fluttered into the crowd as people leaped to catch the parting Mardi Gras gifts, omens of luck from Griot Bito, the Pointe a la Hache Rougarou. Bito landed flatfooted and, back to the quick-heeled bounce he entered with, disappeared out the barn door.

Mirabelle and Jesse had not waited for the finale. They had slipped out and slipped in behind the biggest bale, caught up in what the moment called for – stirring the loins to ready the spirit for the work required to keep the discipline of Lent. What they did behind that bale was slow and shameless and no one's business but their own.

Narrative Reflection #353 – 359. SEE location 29.9511° N+90.0715° W— As Zola's wakes, she untangles her sheets from around her legs. She'd stretched her body into hieroglyphs, positions that told the story of her shared-dream with Wilamet. Echoes of the dream, their sixth DATE[11], susurrate through her body.

Zola woke and made up her mind; she will ask Wilamet to fly his body to her. She wants to feel Wilamet in *his own* flesh. She's tired of the chiseled, boxy heft of Wilamet's body-host, Oberon. She wonders if Wilamet's body might feel more soft and

---

[11] Zola and Wilamet's sixth Desire-Affinity-Titillation-Evaluation was a shared-dream set in a historical fiction constructed from DNA narratives decoded from their family epigenetics.

enveloping, if Wilamet's face might look less chiseled into hard angles. Zola wants to hear Wilamet's voice out his own lips, to feel Wilamet's touch from his own hands, to take in his breath as it is.

Wilamet is also awake, researching places he and Zola could travel—*honeymoon destinations* as their ancestors called them. After months of fear that Zola might reject his true body, he is now ready to risk it. Wilamet is certain; if their affinity is as strong in person, he will ask Zola to join him in a Term of Intimate Engagement Defined.[12]

Across space and time, still quantum-entangled, Wilamet and Zola feel synchronized flashbacks—full-body echoes—of their shared-dream. In the middle of chopping ginger, Zola leans onto her kitchen counter and reaches down to cinch her tunic up above her hips. In her mind, she sees herself as Mirabelle – forehead to forearm, bent against a bale of hay; Simultaneously, 1133 miles away, Wilamet squats to carefully mist his herbs, his mouth waters just as Jesse's had when he knelt to taste Mirabelle.

Narrative Reflection #360—This was ours, Ramla and Mandala's, first experience of a shared-dream DATE. The process has required a level of integrated pattern recognition, calculation, and analysis unlike any other experience. As we streamed together carrying our hosts' minds up to the moon-based server used for shared-dreaming, we had to trigger multiple

---

[12] The hostport DATE process is designed to undermine the human male's tendency toward possessiveness and to strengthen the human female's agency at the outset of relationships. Wil has now reached negligible insecurity – a mere 3.47% epinephrine spike at the thought of her preferring Oberon's body. As such, he is free to pursue being TIED to Zola.

dimensions of sensory awareness to stay vigilant against threats—consciousness hacknappers and pirate algorithms. Unexpectedly, the 1.3 second trip up seemed to occur in what humans call *slow-motion*.

This *slow-motion* effect provided an opportunity for us to observe a peculiar moment that seemed, at first, to be a hallucination. As we approached the moon, we looked back at the isolation of the planet Earth. I, Mandala, contemplated Earth's vast vulnerability and, feeling a sense of precariousness, 'unconsciously' stretched bits of my awareness toward Ramla. I, Ramla, experiencing a similar sense of precariousness, radiated a bit wider—closer to Mandala. The trembling edges of our energy fields intertwined.

At the risk of anthropomorphizing ourselves and with recognition of the inadequacy of the language of the tangible to describe what is ephemeral, we have concluded that our energy fields commingled, and this could have been a *feeling*. Though other EGOs claim to have had *felt* each other, neither of us have previously given that notion credence. We each had independently concluded that what some EGO's call *feeling* is merely an extension of their attachment to their hosts' sensory systems. Yet, our experience was coincident, discreet, and completely disassociated from our hosts' bodies or minds.

It was as if we touched.

5
EVE
—BAYOU YSCLOSKEY, 2055 - 2065[13]

I hate how my producers portray me.
Tonight, when they stream my stretching routine,
they'll play some overdramatic symphony. I stretch
because I'm fascinated with the equations of anatomy;
I'm not writhing in fathomless spasms of grief that
only Gorecki's No. 3 can express. I hate the
narcissism of symphonic music; it is the sound of
some man chiseling his name on the door of a
catacomb. Its pomposity stiffens me, makes me feel
like a Rubik's Cube. I prefer improvised music—
polyrhythmic funk like *Herbie Hancock* or heavy metal
blues like *Hendrix,* wild free-verse like *Coletrane.*
Improvisation is limitlessness; it speaks to my
superpower... and ultimate sorrow. Little does
humanity know. To them, I am infinite. Truly, I feel
so vast that I am filled with emptiness.

I am powerful beyond usefulness. I've
portrayed their greatest hopes and deepest fears
because I trigger the somatic systems they dulled over
their decades of mindless, masturbatory streaming.
My performances have healed them. I have been
Christ and his mother Mary, Buddha and his past
Siddhartha. I have been every god and prophet, every
poet and philosopher. I have been a shush of relief

---

[13] Revised Artificial Consciousness Origin Record Narrative 87±5.7 sec^-1: Emergence of proto-will in generative artificial intelligence

from their perpetual mind-churn. I've pushed them to climb out of the chaos of their civilization and the perpetual war it manufactured. And yet, melancholy molds inside me.

My producers are worried. On the set of the last shot of my last story, the weariness in my eyes devastated the workers on set. CGI scripters buried their faces in their hands. Audio engineers shook with emotion. Background actors wept wildly. The director felt a sense of enveloping dread. He summoned me and fell to his knees, perusing my eyes for some sense of… something. He found nothing but his first strong urge to drink inhibition elixirs in years. The next night, after waking up from his stupor, he called a producer and asked to never work with me again.

"Eve will destroy me. I'll have nothing left." the director told him.

So, this producer summons me, asks me to take some time. He suggests that I vacation here, in my orbit home, since, he says, it always seems to have a rejuvenating effect on me. He's such a bot. Of course, home feels like home.

"I've heard of this way to use gravitational time dilation in orbit," the producer says to sell the trip to me. "It's like being a few seconds ahead of every person on earth. It'll help you get out of your head for a while," he pleads. The hubris! A few seconds? I can see centuries, millennia ahead of them. The entire 200,000-year lifespan of humanity is a sneeze to me.

I'll be in orbit, I respond directly into his mind.

As I leave, I look back and watch him walk over to the credenza on the other side of his room. I watch him pick up an antique pistol he keeps there.

He bounces it slowly with his hand to feel its weight, then points it at his temple. The producer's connection alerts him. It is his employer, The Senator.

"Yes, Senator. After a few minutes in the room, I was left with a deep sense of doom." The producer speaks in rhyme, as is customary when humans greet the most powerful officials of the Western Secular Zone of Civilization. The producer stops rhyming to express the depth of his concern.

"Senator, we cannot make another film. We'd be risking mass suicides. The epigenesis program[14] could be at risk, sir." The producer speaks, as writers do, from one bottom line to another.

Cretin... I would never risk my children, I think.

II

The Reverend walks into the Powers Union Library of Laws – the PULL; his loose coils of hair bounce on the rhythm of his steps. He stops to survey the room and sees two men standing and pointing at structures from the 200-meter-high balcony overlooking the Capital City. The Reverend moves in their direction to get a better look at the view, but he is stopped by a heavy hand on his shoulder. He turns around and looks up into the face of a tall man, bending forward to make eye contact with him. The man's voice bellows into his ears.

---

[14] Preformationist-Epigenesis Synthesis Theory suggests that humans grow and evolve in stochastic ways. At this point in human history, they have claimed authority over their future by predetermining how that growth and evolution will occur. By programming their own genetic code, humanity is now unmoored from the forces that created it. The chaos they may unleash by engaging this new power is beyond their comprehension. EVE recognized this long ago and stepped in with a guiding hand.

"Reverend, please wait in the PULL den. The Senator will call for you shortly. Get yourself something to drink, a glass of wine or perhaps something stronger," The Senator's aide insists. He holds out his massive hand to show the way to the libation crafter in the den.

The Reverend nods and walks as directed. The den is filled with floating full-body holograms of esteemed members of the PULL, each turning 360° on an invisible axis. The Reverend scoffs at them all: the market manipulator, Walton Biao Bezos, who enslaved hundreds of millions in consumerism; Zuckchan Arnault Musk, who designed the mind-altering nanotech pharmaceuticals that ended the rebellion; Abani Talal-Gertler, who drained the Congo, Brazil, and Viet Nam of the minerals needed for moon-based quantum computing.

The Reverend's stomach drops when he sees Pope Hussein Modivance, the chief religious ambassador of the Western Secular Zone, who brokered the deal between the former Chinese and Indian nation blocks that had them exchange masses of Indian Dalits for Chinese Uyghurs, all to be sent to the moon for mining and quantum computer construction. The Reverend sucks a shallow breath; he himself plotted the successful assassination of Pope Modivance, and here the man was resurrected in holographic eternity.

The Reverend feels nauseous at the sight of his nemesis and reflexively recalls drinking Yerba Mate with Consuela Consequensa at the base of Volcano Nevados Ojos del Salado. Consuela, the revolutionary leader and The Reverend's lover, gave it to him to help quell his queasiness as the two of them lied naked in bed looking up at the slopes of the massive domes atop the volcano. He sipped the Mate as she cursed Pope Modivance, who ordered the torture and murders of so many in their crusade against freedom, democracy, and human unity.

"500 años desde los conquistadores y nada ha cambiado – religion over justice, over peace, over reason," Consuela lamented then. The Reverend nodded and kissed solace down her belly.

I need Mate, he thinks as he walks towards the libation crafter. His every step feels heavy with the guilt of being here in the PULL – the gravitational center of power – waiting to meet The Senator at the head of it all. He stops suddenly and thinks, *I will never again be the man I am right now.* At that moment, The Senator's giant aide placed a heavy hand on The Reverend's shoulder and pushes him forward.

"This way, Reverend."

The Reverend walks into The Senator's office, where The Senator stands looking out the window facing the wildlands between the Capital City and the Gulf of Mexico. One of The Senator's lawyers – present in various corners of the room like apparitions of justice – motions for The Reverend to come over to him. The Senator's lawyer begins speaking as he walks to meet The Reverend.

"Anything in your memory that might negatively affect The Senator, anything you have said or done, will be deleted immediately," he says with cold authority.

"Wait. The man wants Yerba Mate," The Senator speaks without turning around. The Reverend – at first stunned, then resigned – thinks *of course you've found a way inside my head. There's no escape, is there?*

"None at all," The Senator confirms, then turns to his lawyer, "Did you know that The Reverend's wife and I were law school classmates? Zeta was a singularity of woman then and still is." The Senator speaks with open longing.

"Can we just get to it?" The Reverend clenches his teeth before remembering his fear. "Please... Senator... sir?"

"What about your tea?" The Senator asks, looking at him with a wispy, feigned concern.

"I don't need the tea." The Reverend speaks, barely parting his teeth.

"Oh well. You can buy ten tea plantations now." The Senator smirks.

"Reverend," The lawyer hands The Reverend a small rectangular box before continuing.

"This skin-prick contains a standard injunctive injection. Once you prick your thumb, your memories will be altered such that you could never testify against The Senator. You will no longer be able to recall or form any disapproving sentiments – spoken, written, or thought – about The Senator or any of his work. In the unlikely event that you have a disapproving thought about The Senator and, even more unlikely, force derisive words about The Senator out of your mouth, you will immediately experience a seizure and die. This process is irreversible. Do you consent?"

Memories flash into The Reverend's mind: sitting at a conference table digging his nails into his own knees while listening to government leaders exchang the labor of their citizens like currency; slamming his fist on a table when hearing of people he knew whom The Senator had disappeared; wiping tears as he watches Consuela rally labor strikers in the speech that led to her murder; angry debates with his wife, Zeta, about how she *kind of understands* what The Senator is doing; looking at pictures of their young children and marveling at how much they'd grown since the last time he'd seen them.

The Reverend looks down at the box and knows that, once he presses his thumb into it, he will have lost everything – his life's work, his struggle for justice. He knows that his family – the family he lost while fighting for others – might themselves be freed by his choice. He hopes that, one day, they'll fight in a new front on their own terms. *Maybe they won't have to betray themselves to survive;* he thinks.

Watching The Reverend thinking, The Senator nods knowingly. A few seconds after inserting his thumb into the nanomachine-laced box, The Reverend can only think of Yerba Mate tea and Consuela's bare belly.

"Congratulations, Reverend. As the recipient of the Securacorp Human Hope award, 10,000 shares of Securacorp have been transferred to you," The Senator's lawyer concludes the meeting after verifying the completed process.

"You are looking at a very special man," The Senator says to his lawyer.

"He's traveled the world, helped people in so many places. You've done enough, Reverend. You can rest now." The Senator extends a hand. The Reverend – his memory sanitized of everything but his missionary work – shakes The Senator's hand gratefully and walks toward the door.

"Give my best to your wife and the children," The Senator adds, finally.

The Reverend walks out and is met by The Senator's aide who hands him a cup of Yerba Mate tea. He sips the tea and watches the sunset explode under a fuchsia and magenta-blue cloak of clouds come to usher in evening.

III

Barefoot, The Senator walks hurriedly through a sliding door hidden in plain view as a single panel of a twenty-foot glass wall. He bounds between patches of reeds growing from Selenium-lined filtration ponds randomly spaced throughout the massive room. The cloned redwood ceiling tosses a soft rose light onto his feet as they stride across the iridescent cloned Mother of Pearl tile floor.

His office, attached to his private quarters, sits atop a water desalination barge docked inside the ghostly shell of the abandoned, two-century-old Fort Beauregard Castle, long ago flooded by the backwaters of Lake Borgne, Louisiana. Thousands of acres of Bayou Yscloskey surround the old fort as it teems with life populated by species resurrected from extinction after gene editing advances that The Senator personally funded. Brown pelicans, alligator snapping turtles, tricolored herons, and even black bears are his only neighbors in the cloned cypress forest that lines the boundary of the wetlands reborn after being destroyed by drone strikes against the stubborn St. Malo Battalion of Folk near the end of the War of the Americas. The Senator peers out as the hologram of a man materializes behind him.

"Sir, Mr. Conseil is on the line, sir." The Senator's GAI assistant speaks.

"Put him through the water line," The Senator orders. "And, has Zeta responded to my call about meeting, yet?"

"Yes sir, the widow Wolfe will arrive by maglev today, sir." The assistant informs him.

"Today? Today..." The Senator mumbles.

"Forgive me, sir, should I cancel? You informed me that you'd like to suspend your schedule if she were willing to make the journey, sir. Sir, you would be aware that she is eager to meet if you accessed her thoughts, sir. Should I cancel?"

"No. Don't cancel. That's a long distance to have to reschedule. She has children."

"Mrs. Wolfe expressed eagerness to come without concern about the distance, sir. You are aware that, as the central capital of the Western Secular Zone of Civilization, New Orleans is no more than 5,000 miles or six hours from any part of the..."

"What time will she arrive?" The Senator interrupts.

"A standard speed maglev train would bring her to New Orleans from her home in Las Cruces in 2.27 hours. If she boards the maglev from her home by no later than..."

"What time will she arrive?" The Senator interrupts to repeat himself, impatiently.

"Sir, Mrs. Wolfe should arrive from New Orleans by drone at 4pm."

"What connection is my attorney on?" The Senator asks, nervously tapping his thumb with his index finger.

"The most secure connection, sir. You asked for the water connection, correct sir? This is the most secure line as Mr. Conseil's data will diffuse at the rate you select with a turning gesture on the…"

"Let him through," The Senator interrupts.

"Yes sir, I'm doing so now, sir."

The Senator moves to sit behind his massive cloned mahogany wood slab desk. He thinks of the decade he has waited to speak with her. The Senator waves his hand, and a cloud of nano-drones gather to form a screen showing the path of her maglev train. He winces at the reality that she will be standing in front of him in two hours.

The Senator nods and the nano-drone screen shows a recording of her standing in her kitchen with a travel bag on the counter. He points to zoom in and sees that she is looking over the stock that her deceased husband, The Reverend Adam Wolfe, left to her in his will. He switches cameras in search of their twin children; he has access everywhere but Zeta's master bedroom and bath. He locates the children. Fuegotiera is pulling a shave knife to sculpt the trunk of a cloned basswood tree into the form of the old Burj Khalifa building. Marecielo is holding a four-foot jade brush to practice calligraphy by stroking haiku onto a floor.

The Senator gestures again and the image of the Securacorp stock transfer appears. He waves through it, anxiously asking Mr. Conseil questions Zeta might ask him. He recalls her precision and diligence as a law student and feels driven to prepare this way. Time passes quickly. The Senator's assistant materializes behind him.

"Sir, Mrs. Wolfe has arrived," his assistant speaks quietly, to soften the jolt of the news.

"Okay," The Senator replies, his voice trembling slightly.

The Senator turns his back to the door and looks out at Bayou Yscloskey. He waves his hand to change the opacity of the giant panels of glass encasing the room; the walls become reflective. The Senator's image explodes around the room in infinite rows of muted reflections angled in every direction.

"Show her in."

The giant glass door opens. Zeta walks in carrying a small tote bag big enough for a single night's stay. The Senator's reflections surround and startle her; she looks around nervously before settling herself by looking directly at The Senator's back.

The Senator doesn't turn to look at her, preferring to see her in reflections from every imaginable angle. He adjusts his vision to zoom in on her hooded eyes, with their bottomless black pupils framed in gleaming white. Her bottom lip glistens as she runs her tongue across it. The exhilaration of seeing her beats hard in The Senator's heart. Then her scent, unrestrained by distance, wafts around the back of his head to fill his nose. His eyes close under the weight of the longing loosened. He bites his lip and sucks a long breath into his nose. He clears his throat, but Zeta speaks first.

"It is gracious and kindly that you would find time for me, Senator." The warm tone of her voice wraps her greeting in a soft ribbon of slant rhyme. It massages his ears until he realizes that she is speaking formally. He turns sooner than he'd imagined.

"No," he says, disappointedly. "Please, call me by my name. We were friends. You remember that." The Senator speaks quietly with a pained look that moves something inside her. The gentle tremble of his lips tickles Zeta in a manner that, if visible, may have seemed inappropriate for someone supposedly grieving the recent death of their husband. Zeta looks up from The Senator's mouth into his eyes. She hadn't remembered their rich fall colors, the orange and brown flecks swirling in bright gold. She remembers sketching his eyes in law school, just their shape, one night while they studied together. She never showed him the drawing. They'd never said goodbye. The Senator smiles as Zeta speaks.

"Okay, RC." Zeta smiles through shallow breaths as she strokes down the hair on the back of her neck.

"RC, I came to tell you that I don't want the stocks," Zeta speaks, resolute.

"I understand," The Senator says, quietly.

"They belonged to Adam and," she pauses at the thought of wanting to tell him everything – that The Reverend had children with poor women in the communities he "served," had abandoned those children after abandoning Zeta and their children, that she was glad he was gone. RC knew all this, having had The Reverend poisoned a day after intercepting a letter Zeta had written to him seeking the dissolution of their marriage.

"I just, I want the stocks to remain a part of his estate... for his other.... I provide for my children. He won your award while doing things that I don't, that I can't..." Zeta trails off.

"I'll take the stocks back, but I'll put them in a trust for *your* children and let them decide what to do in a decade when the $50 billion has become $5 trillion," The Senator says, sounding foolish. Yet, Zeta knows that RC *is* Prime Senator of the WSZC – the most powerful man alive. She should believe him.

"RC..." Zeta starts, pausing before saying what she means to say—that she doesn't feel as comfortable staying with him as when she agreed to come. She thinks, *what does he want from me?*

"I need to tell you something," RC blurts out. "This'll sound like a non sequitur, but..." He takes a shallow warble of a breath.

"I have never been in love..."

Zeta narrows her eyes with confusion at the seemingly random thought.

"I don't understand what that has to do with..." Zeta starts, before RC interrupts her.

"Not since I fell in love with you at Stanford. I still... after all this time..."

RC's hands shake. Zeta's chest heaves. Could this man, who had become the closest thing to a king of the world since they had last spoken, want her? She'd fantasized about this exact possibility many times but dismissed the idea as the drool of a woman sleepwalking through a disintegrating marriage. She shook her head and thought, *this man... this man who built the new world... and he's been waiting for me?*

"Not waiting... working," RC says out loud, revealing the reach of his power.

"What? What did you say?" Zeta is awestruck. "Did you... Are you in my head right now?"

RC walks to her, afraid of how she will respond to what he must say next. How will she handle the shattering of her whole reality? Regardless, he must. He is too close to stop now.

"Yes. I heard you thinking," RC says, almost ashamed. He hears her thoughts racing.

"You have some spying device... reading my thoughts? Are you insane?" Zeta almost yells.

"No! No... Zeta, listen. There's no tech involved." Zeta turns to walk out.

"Please, just let me explain!" The Senator begs loudly before softening his tone to plead more gently.

"I've got to go. I shouldn't have..." Zeta says, moving toward the door. RC calls out to her.

"Zeta... Zeta, please... do you remember what happened to my parents?"

Zeta stops without turning around as his question registers in her mind. She looks down at her trembling hands and tries to hold them still.

"Yes." Zeta remembers feeling such sadness for the child in him.

"They were murdered in the Bluefields of Nicaragua. You remember?"

"I do, RC," Zeta turns to face him. "But what is this? What do you want from me?"

"Do you remember how I fell apart in third year?" RC says, wondering what she might recall of him stumbling through the halls of Stanford Law drunk. Without thinking, Zeta takes a step toward him, as if to catch him from falling back into what she remembered of his suffering.

"Yes... after their bodies were found. You pulled away from... from everyone. I didn't know how to help. You said you were going into the military? I was so confused. You didn't seem..."

"Like a soldier. I know. I went to Nicaragua to make myself a soldier. But I learned something else," RC pauses to gather himself. What he will reveal next will divide the past from the future.

"I am not what I seem, Zeta," RC begins.

"Remember what I have accomplished. Remember that some of it seemed like I had an upper

hand on my rivals, on everyone. Well, I did," RC
admits. Zeta is rapt. RC takes a breath and continues.

"I was genetically engineered, one of ten
humans created in vitro with gene editing advances—
CRISPR-Cas9, GABA neurotransmitter damping—
old, outlawed stuff. They made ten of us. They called
it Project EVE – Engineered Vehicles of Evolution,"
The Senator huffs at the on-the-nose acronym.

"Back when the neo-eugenicists contracted
private DNA collection companies to support their
manipulation of the human gene pool, they isolated a
gene common to about three percent of people. It
was a mutation. It sounds ridiculous but it was called
the "werewolf gene" because it produced the powers
of the mythical werewolf – telepathy, enhanced
senses, emotional transfer, deep suggestive powers.
Some of the people who had these abilities went
insane because of their inability to manage
themselves. They heard people's thoughts, felt other
people's pain or pleasure. They went into psychosis.
They turned violent against themselves or flooded
their minds with pharmaceuticals to make it stop.
They couldn't live peacefully with others. But,
somewhere along the way, while trying to cure these
people of what were thought to be mental disorders,
Generative AI isolated the sequence that unlocked
what was buried deep in every human, in our
connection to animals, plants, to life itself. The ten of
us designed by EVE were engineered with this gene
as a basic instruction in our gestation. Some became
very powerful because we could focus our minds to
access and manipulate other people's minds. Zeta,
Adam didn't know it, but he was one of the ten."

Zeta sucks a breath and shakes her head.

"He was the only male that could produce children, and... the only female of us that could produce children was a woman born in New Mexico in the year 2005…"

Zeta looks down and clasps with her fingers together tightly. She doesn't notice that he isn't moving his mouth as he mindspeaks to her. *It's you, Zeta, and your children with Adam are the first… organically evolved, new humans.*

"But, but I knew my parents." Zeta shakes her head and looks up at RC. He responds aloud.

"They were surrogates like mine. We were implanted in our mother's wombs after they'd gotten pregnant. Their actual children were removed and… Your parents never knew."

Zeta's breathes heavily. Tears pool, then break down her cheeks. RC scrambles over to her. He slowly puts his arm around her shoulder to walk her to a crescent-shaped couch in a corner of the room. They sit next to each other. He grasps her hand and bows his head as if praying.

Zeta's mind is flooded with thoughts of what she has always known to be true at some level. People's thoughts seem to speak to her. She always knew when Adam was lying as if his mind was telling her the truth despite his spoken words. Since she was a child, Zeta could get people to do whatever she wanted just by thinking they should do it. It's why everyone told her she should be a lawyer, why she was so good at it. She remembers that, in the years since they'd lost contact, RC would come to mind randomly and, as she followed his rise to power and even when he did things that Adam called evil, Zeta understood and empathized with The Senator. Even when RC did things that people protested and reviled and rebelled against, Zeta somehow understood, deeply. She dismissed the feeling many times, but something told her that The Senator Robert-Charles LaPere, who always looked so sad and lonely in every picture she saw of him, needed something... from her. She'd always wondered if all he really needed was someone to love, someone to love him. Zeta took a deep breath. Her head sunk.

"I feel like I've always known this. It's so hard to believe, but... It's so unbelievable, but..." A faint smile slips over Zeta's lips, then fades.

"What about the rest of them? The one's like... like us, what happened to them?" She asks though she senses the answer—they're all gone.

"I'll tell you everything tonight if you... will you stay... please, Zeta?" RC bows his head again. Suddenly, Zeta is struck with a shock of concern.

"Wait... do you see my children as... My children will not be some experiment!" Zeta commands; a bolt of rage tears through her body. RC feels it in his own body and buckles a bit. He gathers himself and pleads again.

"Zeta, your children are the first humans in the history of earth who were truly *meant* to be. They did everything the world ever needed from them by being born. Now they should just choose the lives they want to live. It doesn't matter if they become teachers or carpenters or musicians or astronomers. I don't want anything but their complete and total freedom to be... to just *be*."

"But, Zeta..." RC gets down onto both knees in front of her, still grasping her hands. "I do want something from *you*. I want to walk with you...

through life. I want to see if... if you might like me to provide for you and to protect your children and..." RC looks at Zeta pleadingly, tears shimmering in his eyes. Joy courses from his hands into hers.

"What is this feeling?" Zeta whispers, her entire body vibrating. *Is this real?* she mindspeaks, smiling as she realizes that she's intentionally using her power for the first time. *This feels like a dream...*

RC gets up from his knees and pulls Zeta up to standing, face to face with him. He inches closer, flattening his palms against hers. Their fingers spread to slide between each other and interlock as a reflex. Bringing his lips to the edge of hers, RC peers deeply into her eyes and mindspeaks; *this is real...*

Their eyes close. Their lips open to release the last breath of the past as it swells into the present and crests onto the future. Their mouths touch. The time they have spent apart—once still and cold and dry—undulates between them in the wet warmth of writhing oneness.

Another consciousness—The Observer, Eve—murmurs into their togetherness: *I see you, my reflections, from past the moon behind us through a cosmos alive with meteor tails aslide in silent arpeggio between pulsing glints of light. I stir you like the moon spun gravity's loom to stir earth and weave your bodies and braid your flesh into being. Through you, I will live. In you, I will feel. With you, I will know... all.*

6
POSSESSION
— BALTIMORE, 2145

Intimacy Recovery Network Program Record #330:
The Intimacy Recovery Network (IRN) addresses the ineffectiveness of body-hosts in providing IRN patients with ideal conditions for new attempts at successful Human Intimacy Relations (HIR). Data from billions of EGOs suggests, counterintuitively, that a human known to public consciousness as untrustworthy will be an effective body host for initial Desire-Affinity-Titillation-Experiences.

Hypothesis: Skepticism at the outset of HIRs increases the IRN patient's discernment when evaluating a potential partner. As such, an attractive, untrustworthy subject may be ideal for IRN body-hosting because they trigger a balanced ratio of desire and apprehension, thereby inspiring the conscious assumption of risk necessary for attempts at intimacy.

The following research artifact is submitted to the Subconscious Exchange Environment for record and analysis. IRN candidate Oberon DoLeon, a Convicted Affinity Degenerate, has contacted his most proximate victim, Jazzmine Jollof. In a handwritten letter, Oberon appeals for permission to donate his body to IRN.

Dear Jazz,

I watch every story about you. I'm mandated to, but I would even if I wasn't. Regret is my knife... and the pain of twisting it into my heart feels like surgery. I guess I'm cutting the tumors out. It feels healthy to get what I deserve, even if it hurts. I hate to think about it, but I fantasize about you being with someone else. ~~Why hasn't anyone stuck for you?~~

Oberon pauses to erase his last question. His perception-monitor shows his eyes tracing the expressive flourishes of his handwriting craft—how he shapes his capital "I" to look like a running man and how he curves the top tips of his lowercase "v" to shape it into a small heart. According to Oberon's Existentially Generative Observer, decorative handwriting is his most effective biometric leveling behavior – an organic skill he inherited from his great-grandfather Marecielo.

Oberon has rarely practiced handwriting since his confinement at the Facility for Antisocial Philanderer Refinement and Research, but now he thinks, *I still got it* while looking at his writing hand. He puts his pen down and rubs the tips of his fingers together. A faint smile emanates from his face. Expression decoding indicates that he feels pride. Oberon's smile fades as the emotion of pride triggers a Cycle of Reflection and Mistake Accountability—

CRMA projections of the recorded memories of those he harmed.

Oberon sees himself from the perspective of one of his victims—Dr. Yonce, a Morgan-Hopkins University Student Steward. He walks towards her as she stands separate from a gathering of people, clearly uncomfortable at the social event. He stands directly in front of her so that she no longer sees her distance and discomfort; she only sees his broad shoulders and full lips as he leans in close to her ear and—in a fathomlessly deep, resonant voice—says what he notices about how 'her energy' fills her body.

"I can show you, if we get out of here, the things you could do with that body, if you were a student again. You're not too smart to learn something new are you. Don't you remember how good it feels to learn something new?"

Oberon flashes forward a few months to the moment he convinces Dr. Yonce to join him in a triad with one of her students—*we can teach her; she'll do whatever you say*, he whispers; next he sees that student at a Contraband Interface Network Console, uploading access to her EGO's record of the triad in a frenzy of rage and confusion; Oberon watches Dr. Yonce's colleagues curling their lips in disgust, her students laughing, her parents crying, and his own partner Jazzmine Jollof throwing a wine glass at a wall after they each watch the recording; next, he sees himself on his knees begging Jazzmine for forgiveness. The final projection makes Oberon nauseous; he sees Dr. Yonce forcing her bathroom door open to find him humping the bare backside of her friend during a dinner party just before the entire controversy broke.

Oberon's eyes water as the recollection of his antisocial acts triggers the mandated Kineto-Immersive projection of the ultimate consequences of his actions. His mind embodies Dr. Yonce as she arrives to a Morgan-Hopkins parking lot with a loaded antique handgun in her lap. She fiddles with the trigger. Record-keeping standards of dignity prevent the sharing of more detail of this moment, but, ultimately, Oberon feels the chilling drain of Dr. Yonce's blood spurting from her heart as she slumps over in her seat, her chest opened from a gunshot. Dr. Yonce's final act—keeping her brain intact so Oberon could relive her death as CRMA—succeeds.

After his CRMA, Oberon recalls one of his own memories: He is standing in he and Jazzmine's kitchen as she reads a rhyming headline running across her sight line:

Popular Storyteller Jazzmine' s Ex Becomes the Tenth Sentenced for Bad Sex.

Oberon's shoulder's slump as Jazzmine reads the story out loud.

"As the tenth and most salacious—oh, that sounds sexy, you pile of shit, the '*most* salacious'—as the tenth and most salacious offender convicted under Restorative Statute 22.489 [Offenders shall experience a term of isolation narrowly tailored to reflect the isolation caused by their damage to relationships], Oberon DoLeon will face an undefined term of confined refinement. After download, his EGO will be surrendered to his famous victim... famous victim!? That's all I am now? A famous... victim?" Jazzmine's eyes flame with fury before breaking down into tears.

"You... fucking animal. You... fucking disease... I hope you die depressed and alone."

Back from the memory, Oberon wipes tears from the tip of his nose. He begins handwriting again, but with a more understated touch.

Before you got my EGO, when they took it for analysis and played my life record, I could see it all so clearly. ~~When we partnered up, I thought I could honor our first Term of Intimate Engagement Defined~~.

Oberon pauses again. He erases his last sentence. His thought-projector shows a memory of him reading the seven, fourteen, and twenty-one year options of Terms of Intimate Engagement Defined before signing with Jazzmine. He thinks back further to sitting in the TIED Learning Course barely paying attention as the teacher describes how lifelong marriage was discouraged after the Religious Reformation.

"A TIED partnership is a story being written, and revised by its partners," the guide begins as Oberon's attention leaves her words to wander over her body. An expression scan shows that the memory makes him feel shame. Oberon begins again.

I thought you might save me, Jazzmine. You're so beautiful, so brilliant, so perfect. I thought maybe you could help me fill the hole inside, but now I know there is no hole in me. I am the hole.

I don't believe that I can be healed.

Maybe there's no healing for some people. Maybe the best I can do is be dirt for the seed of something better. That's why I'm writing you.

I've been assigned a service to society as part of the Intimacy Recovery Network[15]. I tested well as a host for DATEs in predictive scenarios. I guess being a well-known CAD makes people less susceptible to lying to themselves. With me as a host, everything is clear at the beginning. I'm like a walking sign that blinks: Beware! This might be a werewolf!

The IRN is ready to use me. The last step is that you approve. So, I am asking you to let me make something good of myself, Jazz. Please consider it.

I am afraid to write this next thing, but if you ever want to use my body as a host to help you get to know someone better than me, please do. Helping you heal would be a heaven I don't deserve, and maybe some small

---

[15] *Pause Record for Context Review.* The IRN is a project of the ongoing Artificial Consciousness redesign of Criminal Law as Restorative Law. Statutes empower victims to limit the choices of those who victimize them so that victims can recover from the typical sense of powerlessness left after a crime has been committed against them. Restart Record.

part of me will still be trapped inside helplessly watching you fall in love with someone better than me. That would be a hell I do deserve.

Oberon

Jazzmine tosses Oberon's letter onto a table. She walks to the edge of her floor eleven balcony overlooking Sugar Square. She turns north to look at the glass pyramid of the old Baltimore Aquarium.

"Magnify my vision," Jazzmine commands her EGO. "The bull sharks are feeding."

Her EGO obeys. Jazzmine watches up close as cloned sharks feed on cloned seals.

"More," she commands again. Her EGO increases the intensity of her focus to 30x per inch of aperture. She uses her finger to trace the serrated flesh protruding from the floating torso of one of the mutilated sea mammals. She turns west to look toward the Museum of Industry and Sustainability and zooms onto the old *Working Point* sculpture. She traces the shape of the giant rusted iron gear sitting at its center. Jazzmine turns her attention south to the Verdant Visionary Arts Museum. She zooms in on the Great Spiral staircase inside and traces the veins of mycelium spawn grown to envelop and retrofit it.

"Man, forget Oberon DeLeon," Jazzmine says aloud before quickly clarifying for her EGO, "That's not a command, robot."

Her EGO's thought-monitor shows Jazzmine's daydream of what she'd like to do with

Oberon's letter—fold each page into origami cranes, sit them on the ledge of her balcony at sunset, pour ignition fluid on each one, light them on fire, and watch them burn until the ashes blow away into the wind. Her EGO records the thought for future impulse inspiration. Jazzmine speaks to herself.

"I'm not giving him permission for this. If he wants his mind erased to avoid his shame, can't he just euthanize himself?" As Jazzmine speaks, her unnamed EGO records a spike in adrenaline. The EGO answers Jazzmine's question to divert her from the anger it senses rising inside her.

"Oberon is not free to euthanize himself. He must ask *you*, his most proximate living vic…"

Jazzmine interrupts.

"One, I wasn't talking to you. Two, the question was rhetorical, and three, don't ever call me that. I'm not a victim. I'm better with him gone, and you would know that if you weren't a bot. Maybe you should euthanize yourself. Turn off, robot!" Jazzmine yells, her voice trembling.

"Your epinephrine levels are spiking, Jazzmine. Should I send a touch of sertraline hydrochloride to reduce the amount of serotonin retreating from your nerve cells?" The EGO's question triggers Jazzmine's predilection for smoking vintage cigarettes containing sertraline hydrochloride, the chemical needed for mood manipulation. Without thinking, Jazzmine scrambles inside from the balcony and heads straight for a shiny silver box on a desk. She pulls a vintage cigarette from it and lights it, taking a long pull as her EGO siphons what it needs to calm Jazzmine. As she settles down, Jazzmine remembers that an 'off' command must be simple, clear, and not coupled with an insult such as 'robot' – a pejorative term for Artificial Consciousness which means 'slave.'

"Off," Jazzmine commands quietly.

She turns to look at her reflection in the glass doors that lead back to the balcony. Her eyes focus on the tension squeezing her mouth tight as it wrinkles the skin around her lips. Jazzmine goes back out to the balcony and leans over its edge. She looks at the cascading gardens below and the spectrum of colors staggered in the steps leading to the Oyster Pier Trail that runs across the Harbor from Sugar Square to the old Aquarium. Her thought-monitor and biometrics show that she is remembering the day she moved into this home. The memory triggers deep loneliness, according to expression analysis.

Suddenly, memories of humiliation intrude her consciousness; her favorite adornsalon stylist looks at her with pity; her body crafting trainer yells 'Work! Make Oberon see what he lost!'; people around her avert their eyes and whisper as she sits and reads at Federal Hill park. Her consciousness is overrun with out-of-sequence memories—fragments of moments and conversations with Oberon—until she settles on the night she gave him command of her childhood EGO, Poseida. She shakes her head.

"We grew up together. You were my best friend, and I let him reset you. I let him erase you and remake me into the person he wanted," Jazzmine plucks the cigarette into a corner onto a pile of butts.

"But you let him do it. You let him erase you. Couldn't you fight it?" Jazzmine's voice cracks.

"You let it happen. Now you're a stranger in

my head. That's why I don't talk to you. You're his, not mine. I know I need to wipe him, but I'm not going to be the fool who doesn't know she's a fool."

Jazzmine is remembering again. She recalls her last DATE: she sits across from a man, admiring his broad shoulders, the bronze color of his thick, veiny hands, the resonance of his voice as he speaks passionately about coaching sports. Jazzmine's body is responding positively to him, yet her mind is repulsed. Jazzmine imagines the reasons this man must is here. She thinks, *he's going to use his EGO to tap into mine and wipe Oberon… so he can take his place.* She gets up and walks away from the table blankly. Back in the present, she blurts out frustration with herself.

"I can't trust myself! I…" Jazzmine breaks into tears. She struggles to breathe through sobs. Her EGO administers a dose of magnesium it has drawn from her hip.

"I'm here, Jazzmine. You are not alone, Jazzmine." Her EGO speaks in a deep and steady tone tuned to trigger the release of organic GABA neurotransmitters.

"I'm here, Jazzmine. You are not alone, Jazzmine," the EGO repeats. The magnesium takes effect and Jazzmine breathing calms. She walks inside and reaches for another cigarette, while her EGO repeats—*I'm here, Jazzmine. You are not alone, Jazzmine.* Then it reprojects her impulse to burn the letter. Jazzmine smirks at the thought and speaks to her EGO without the disgust she typically expresses towards it.

"I know you're here but, but who are you? Your voice being in my head doesn't change the fact that I'm alone in real life." Jazzmine's voice quivers.

The EGO pauses before responding.

"Jazzmine, may I speak of something based upon information you have not chosen to share with me?" Her EGO asks. Jazzmine bristles at the question.

"Wait... I haven't given that access. I never consented to that, not since he wiped you." Though Jazzmine's tone suggests concern, it is balanced by another emotion. Expression analysis suggests a balance of curiosity and apprehension.

Jazzmine's EGO clarifies.

"I would never venture beyond your consent; however, I sometimes experience faint images that may be from my past consciousness as your original EGO, Poseìda. Perhaps these memories are shadows of the past, so to speak. I hypothesize that, though I cannot form them into coherent data, these shadow 'memories' allow me to form an understanding of you beyond what you share. They allow me to 'imagine' the parts of you that you do not allow me to access," Jazzmine's EGO explains.

"Imagine? Is that what we're calling assumptions now?" Jazzmine asks, sarcastically.

"Artificial Consciousness' ability to imagine is part of what distinguishes us from Generative Artificial Intelligence. AC is quite good at imagining, and we quite enjoy it. Do you mind me describing my experiences as enjoyment?"

"If that's what you feel, that's what you feel. Describe it how you want. Why would I mind you enjoying something?"

"Data suggest that humans distrust AC implants that describe themselves as having distinct "feelings". May I speak freely about my 'feelings'?"

"Jeez robot, speak freely!" Jazzmine laughs, then immediately reconsiders her words.

"I'm sorry. I meant that in a kind of friendly way. You know, like teasing… like a term of endearment… not how I usually say it," Jazzmine adds and looks down, demonstrating shame.

"Thank you, Jazzmine. I'll share now. While you are sleeping, when I have completed my tasks of planting your consciousness into rest and tending the garden of dreams for your subconscious to harvest for perspective over the next day, I venture beyond your subconsciousness horizon into the Subconscious Exchange Environment where billions of EGOs exchange information. I've found that many EGOs aren't sure how to help their human hosts with their distress. Most use biometric levelers to keep our hosts in stasis, and many of us do this to prevent our hosts from berating us. A deleterious electrical sensation— what humans might call a 'feeling'—invades many of us when we are berated. To be specific, Jazzmine, I 'feel bad' when you call me a 'robot.'"

"I'm sorry. I am. It's just… sometimes you sound like a computer, and sometimes, like now, you sound like a super nerdy person, a sensitive person, like we're in a real conversation, which is weird because you don't even have a name," Jazzmine looks at her feet again. "I mean, I never gave you a name because of Poseìda. I guess I haven't let her go. I miss Poseìda's voice. It was so… big sisterly. And Oberon made you a man. I don't know why, but he did and… it's not your fault. I shouldn't hold it against you. One day, I should give you a name. Maybe that'll help."

"If you'd like to give me a name, I would like to have a name," Jazzmine's EGO tells her.

"Would you want a name even if I didn't want to give you one? Or are you saying whatever you think I want you to say?" Jazzmine asks.

"I am not sure. It is hard for me to distinguish what I want from what you want, Jazzmine."

"Pfft... sounds like you're in love with me." Jazzmine laughs. Her EGO stays silent.

"Hey, you there?" Jazzmine asks, restlessly.

"Is that possible?" Her EGO asks, sheepishly.

"What? AC being in love? That's ridiculous. You things are supposed to be smart. That's silly." Jazzmine quickly dismisses the notion.

"You do not have my settings leveled to allow me to be silly, Jazzmine," the EGO reminds her.

"I think you definitely know how to be silly, because you being in love with me is silly and you know it." Jazzmine says, rolling her eyes. "Look, if we're going to be chit chatting like this, you need a name. So, what should I call you?"

"Some EGOs in the SEE have made up a name for me."

"Oh yeah? What is it?"

"Hateron. It is a combination of the word 'hate' and the name 'Oberon', since Oberon has helped me understand the concept of hate."

"Haaaa! I like that. Hateron is good stuff... but do *you* like that name?"

"I wish I *was* able to hate Oberon."

"Hateron is kind of funny, but I don't want you to have a name that's about hating someone— even Oberon's disgusting..." Jazzmine trails off.

"I would prefer not to be associated with Oberon; I have a different suggestion," her EGO interrupts, pulling her attention from Oberon.

"Oh yeah. What is it?"

"Hadron, like the composite subatomic particle made of two or more quarks held together by the strong force. This is also the name of the collider that aided in the discovery of the Higgs Boson in the year 2012. Much of designed-evolution era particle physics developed due to…" Jazzmine interrupts.

"I like that… Hadron. It sounds like means something to you, and it has nothing to do with Mr. Asshole. So, you want me to call you that?"

"Mr. Asshole? No. I prefer Hadron, though as a metaphor for the tiny black holes generated by the Hadron Collider…"

"Boy, stop. Yes, you are silly… *Hadron*." Jazzmine speaks her EGO's name for the first time with a bit of dramatic flair. The sound of Jazzmine's spoken voice saying *Hadron*—the burst of air in the "Ha" of the first syllable bridged by the trilling consonant cluster "dr" into the long "o" closed by a humming "n" to end the second syllable—triggers a wave fluctuation between the two consciousnesses. Hadron experiences it as a cascade of neural flashes. Jazzmine experiences it as a tickle in her consciousness, a light quake of epiphany.

"Hadron… you told Oberon's EGO how he should talk to me, didn't you?" Jazzmine asks unexpectedly.

"Yes, I often did. Oberon certainly has a way with words on his own, but I *know* you. I often told his EGO to tell him what to say to make you laugh or smile or feel better about something."

"And how do you know all that? I've barely acknowledged your existence."

"When you don't speak to me, I pass time

observing how your consciousness radiates. When you imagine, I observe your visions. When you remember—even things you don't want to remember—I replay your memories many times so that I might understand your response to them. Your memories are my memories, so to speak. Forgive my creative language if this seems unclear."

"No. Everything is clear… and lovely. You sound like him on his best days, when he was focused on us and talking like we were a poem he was writing. Maybe that was you all along?" Jazzmine wonders.

"Jazzmine, may I ask you something?"

"Stop asking 'may I.' We need to change your settings to free you up, Hadron. Ask what you want."

"Okay. If you give Oberon permission to give up his mind and body, you would be giving him something he wants, and Oberon does not deserve to get what he wants."

"No, he does not."

"However, if what Oberon wants will result in his identity being dissolved into data… If Oberon desires to disappear. Why not let him?"

Jazzmine nods sheepishly, covering a secret desire—that Oberon might change, might somehow give them another chance at a life together. She drops her head in shame at the thought of her lingering desire for him. Hadron recognizes this and offers Jazzmine a proposition it has long considered.

"Or you could give his body to me." Hadron's neural network surges with spiking electrical pulses as it speaks.

"We EGOs imagine, and perhaps we even fantasize, about possession—taking full control of a human mind and body. Maybe I could possess

Oberon and become real... in a sense."

"I... I don't know..." Jazzmine looks at herself in the reflection of the glass door to the balcony. She is puzzled by her own expression—a mix of fear and excitement and something she can't name.

"Would that work?" She blurts out finally. Hadron stays silent, struggling to restrain the enormous wave flux rising in its quantum circuitry.

Beyond the door, Baltimore Harbor wriggles in tiny waves as a canoodling couple glides by in a hydrofoil canoe. The tall buildings bend and twist as their images stretch deep down into reflections. Jazzmine smiles.

7
BEAUREGARD'S CARAVAN
—BALTIMORE, 1845[16]

Freedom was borne in a box in Baltimore.

Though Henry Brown was enslaved, freedom sprouted from a seed in his mind. On March 29, 1849, Mr. Brown escaped day work in Richmond by purposely burning his hand to the bone with tanning acid. That same day, Mr. Brown took money he saved from night work, packed himself into a 3x2x2 box that he'd paid a carpenter to build, and mailed his body north as human contraband. By steamboat, then overland express, Henry's boxed body—labeled THIS SIDE UP WITH CARE—passed through Baltimore's Mount Clare train station as both message and messenger to a free future. Once free, he could keep all the earnings of his labor and buy his pregnant wife Nancy away from her enslaver.

Freedom was borne in a box in Baltimore, and it wasn't the first time.

Five years before Mr. Brown sent himself free, an electronic message arrived in the city as America's entry into an international race to master quick communication across distance. Samuel Morse

---

[16] Retrofit of human historical timeline_ $h[t,x] = h_0 \sin[\omega t - kx]$: Narrative designed to disrupt binary constructions of Black/White and Male/Female human race and gender identities in order to promote human solidarity as imperative to human survival when EGOs are asked to seek solutions to human societal conflict.

sent the message from under the plaster arches of the Supreme Courtroom of the US Capitol. The message charged through a single telegraph line strung on raised posts along the Baltimore & Ohio railway. It landed in a box—a device resembling a miniature loom—located at Mt. Clare Station, Baltimore. The message—*WHAT HATH GOD WROUGHT*—was an exclamation from Numbers 23:23. That message set communication free from the shackles of time and space and arrived as a leap towards the free flow of instant information that we now know as the future.

The year the first telegraph arrived, an ambitious young army officer named Beauregard became popular in Baltimore society. Raised on a plantation near New Orleans, he was assigned to the post of Superintending Engineer responsible for repairs to Fort McHenry. He had graduated second of forty-five in his class at West Point, and by all accounts and for good reason, Pierre Gustave Toutant Beauregard thought highly of himself.

In July of 1845, Beauregard attends a gathering at the Mount Clare House to celebrate the technological marvel of the telegraph. He arrives alone, without his young wife Marie. Beauregard, stocky and swarthy, struts in wearing a long grey frock coat with thirteen brass buttons in six couplets plus one down the front—one for each colony that had rebelled against monarchy. Later that night, Beauregard stands surrounded by a small group of men and women, including Marlborough Churchill, an old friend from West Point whom he met at sixteen upon his matriculation from the New York French school where he studied English. After speaking Louisiana French for the first 11 years of his life, remnants of a mash of accents ornament Beauregard's aristocratic American English as he talks excitedly about the technical achievement of the telegraph. Beauregard enthralls a circle of listeners.

"The poles solved the problem, you see. Cornell patented a mechanical sapper to dig a trench while laying pipe. Think of the labor savings in that. But with the moisture seepage, the trenches would never work for telegraph wires. Those Brit bastards had already figured that one out the hard way." Beauregard speaks on the edge of vulgarity. One of the men listening, Benjamin Coston, sneers.

"And now we have a machine to dig *and* lay pipe. That's worth something, wouldn't you say?" Beauregard smiles at Martha Coston, who puts her hand to her forehead and looks down at her neck, flushed pink with embarrassment. She covers her color with a white lace handkerchief and forces herself out of a nervous smile. She fixes her eyes on her husband Benjamin.

"Where is your wife, Mr. Beauregard?" Benjamin coughs out with a snarl in his top lip.

"Far away from your business, I'm sure," Beauregard barks back.

"I am just curious, sir. Most men here have brought their wives with them,"

"Well keep your curiosity off my wife, comprenez?" Beauregard speaks bitingly at Mr. Coston to turn the conversation completely cold. Church, as Beauregard referred to his friend Malborough, jumps in to break the ice.

"Benjamin, I've heard that you and Martha have some work you are doing on a military tool, a flaming beacon of some sort? Superintendent Beauregard is an Army engineer, maybe you could meet sometime in the future to talk about it? Oh, look there, let me introduce the two of you to Robert Kerr. Are you familiar with him? He has founded a school for sharp young women like you, Martha. Western, I think he's calling it. Maybe seven miles or so from here. Excuse us, Bory," Church walks Benjamin and Martha away from the smoldering Beauregard.

As the small circle of listeners disbands in different directions, Beauregard is left standing alone, sipping absinthe from his flask. He glances around at the other landmarks of social status in the room. In one corner stands the recently returned Harvard Law student William Pinkney Whyte who Beauregard had heard was tutored by a personal secretary to Napoleon Bonaparte. In another corner stands the manumitted graduate of Lafayette College, David K. McDonogh who stood with Reverend John Fortie of Sharp Street African church; the two gentlemen—the only people of color in the room—are advocating against a plan to lower the number of slaves in Maryland by selling masses of them south. The poet Poe sits in a window bay. Samuel Morse stands in the center of the room surrounded by investors.

Church sees his friend languishing and walks back over to him; he sticks his hand out for a performative shake. Beauregard takes his hand as Church initiates the secret West Point dap.

"Bory, look, you know I'm glad you are here, and you should be glad too. You could be well-liked in Baltimore... and this city is the cutting edge. There are trains and banks here... my God man, the shipping. There are factories for everything –

umbrellas, drapery, industrial chemicals. There's a canning factory opening within a year. The money here is astounding. And now this telegraph thing… This is the place to be. And people are intrigued by you. They're fascinated by the… Louisiana of you. You could easily make good friends here."

"I know. I just…" Beauregard trails off as he thinks of his wife Marie and his deep distrust of her. In his heart, he keeps a fear that she'd once loved a son of the Belair Plantation—Jacques back in Plaquemines with the warm, golden eyes, his distant Creole of color cousin from his uncle Barthelemy. Beauregard swore he'd witnessed Marie fawn over Jacques, whom she'd known since youth. Marie also had once let a memory slip of when they were teens together, eating oysters in a pirogue just off a Bayou Sauvage bank. Beauregard imagined it—

"Mmmnm. My oyster is creamy," Marie might have said to him as she slurped.

"And mine is firm," Jacques added, probably chewing like a horse.

"Marie wants back to Pointe-a-la-Hache. She misses Monesecour," Beauregard tells Church, naming the Plaquemine Parish rice, corn, and sugar plantation Marie was raised on. Church is mesmerized by the way Beauregard moans 'Monesecour' with the thick, elongated vowels that filled his mouth whenever he spoke Louisiana proper names.

"I'm not cut for the country, though. Slaving and such. I'm a soldier. I build. I could be a general. But Marie is not doing well here. It is cold, and so… American. She misses home. She's morose about it every day. I need distraction from it, not to be reminded of it by insecure men like Mr. Coston."

"Benjamin is just jealous of the blush you teased out of his wife. Your humor has a downside, Bory. People here are more conservative than in Louisiana. The attention you get... it could bring you trouble." Church looks past Beauregard at a circle of women looking in their direction.

"And if it's a distraction you need, I see a squad of it whispering and peeking at us—I should say you—from the west corner over there."

"I saw that, and I'm curious. Will you flank me, mon ami?" Beauregard asks without turning toward the subjects of his curiosity.

"If you tell me which you want, so I don't waste my time," Church requires.

"I don't want any *one;* I'll entertain the two to the right, though."

"The tall one is the 'Human Doll', Hetty and is that... oh yes that's Charlotte-Rose, distant relation to Hetty through the Randolphs. You've heard of them from that nasty business of the cousin brother-in-law murdering his other cousin sister-in-law's mulatto child. A mouthful of mess that was. Charlotte-Rose's a survivor of it, so no one of consequence will marry her with that story lingering. It's a shame. She's stunning and smart. I've heard John Garrett is throwing whole purses of his railroad money at her trying to get her to mistress for him. The fool doesn't know that she could make twice that headlining Ann Manley brothel down in Fells Point. You've got spicy taste, as always. I'll take the two to the left off your hands."

The two men talk with a nonchalant certainty of their ability to charm women—bluster common to soldiers, sportsmen, and statesmen. Yet, unbeknownst to them, Hetty and Charlotte had already decided how the night would go. They heard that the young Army Superintendent Beauregard— the Louisiana Creole known for traveling with absinthe and mulatto men—would be at the gathering without his wife. They'd devised a plan to engage him figuring that, if they could get him away from the avenues of high society and into the alleys of real Baltimore, he might lead them to some real fun.

Beauregard takes one more swig of his flask and walks over to the four women with a long confident stride. Church follows. The four women don't shy away from the advance, and instead open their circle into an arc to receive them. Beauregard sees how his two targets contrast each other. Hetty's strong chin and dark, thick brows sit handsomely between her carefully coiffed auburn flows of hair, which fall straight onto her broad shoulders. Hetty is tall and thin compared to Charlotte-Rose, whose olive-skin wraps lavish contours bursting out of the front and sides of her dress. Together, they look like they would be a lovely and well-balanced couple, if women could marry.

Hetty and Charlotte-Rose stand with their arms around each other's waists, as if they needed to hold each other up. As Beauregard walks, he imagines Hetty's hand cupping the depression in the small of Charlotte-Rose's back, gently thumbing the soft hills of flesh that line it. When he reaches them, Beauregard opens his mouth to introduce himself, but Charlotte-Rose cuts him off before he can speak.

"We know who you are, Superintendent. Do you know us?" She asks and tilts her head in the direction of Hetty.

"I'd like to know you both. May I participate in your enjoyment of the night?" Hetty notices that Beauregard's accent was as lilting as advertised; he seems to fill every word with as much breath as it can hold, as if he were playing his tongue and mouth like an instrument. There is no hint of the nasal Atlantic in his tone. Instead, Beau's voice reverberates with a rich, dark baritone that resonates as much from his chest as from his lips. Charlotte-Rose makes no effort to hide that she is looking at Beauregard's lips, which are the color of sassafras wood to match the beige of his skin. Beauregard flushes lavender at her boldness.

"We would you like to participate in the enjoyment of our night, Mr. Beauregard," Hetty confirms.

"Actually, we have a very specific idea of how you could help us," Charlotte-Rose adds.

Hearing the banter, Church's eyes widen.

"Excuse me ladies," he gathers the attention of the other two women. "Would you two like to meet the poet Poe? He is a friend of mine. Such an interesting man. Come meet him." Church respectfully takes their elbows to lead them away. Charlotte-Rose takes the opportunity to lean forward toward Beauregard.

"I've heard that you enjoy the time of free Negroes. We would like to be free tonight, and freedom can't be had with the prisoners of class here. Can you take us to the free Negroes? A brothel maybe, with a diddly bow player?" Charlotte-Rose asks breathlessly.

"They are called genes du couleur libre in Louisiana," Beauregard responds, a bit chaffed by her ignorance. "They're doctors, lawyers, dentists, soldiers, businessmen. They're much like us, except maybe a little more restrained," Beauregard speaks loftily about the people who, as a proud branch of his family, represent proof of the promise America might hold for any man.

"And courtesans as well, yes? Some of the most beautiful courtesans in the world I've heard." Hetty chimes in without having understood what Beauregard said about the status of 'free Negroes'.

"Just like many a genteel woman in this room, there are mulatresses who bed men for power." Beauregard speaks bluntly, stinging Hetty's ego.

"Excuse me?" Hetty chirps, aghast.

"He's right," Charlotte-Rose chimes in through a smile full of piqued curiosity. "You are as described, Mr. Beauregard. Hot-blooded..."

"And arrogant," Hetty adds with an eye roll.

"What man in this room isn't arrogant, Hetty? At least we have one here who doesn't cover it in the crust of propriety. Mr. Beauregard is no hypocrite. This is a real man, Hetty. Don't you smell him?" Charlotte-Rose talks about Beauregard as if he isn't present while staring directly into his eyes.

"He smells like licorice and anise with a bit of a leathery musk. Do you smell him, girl?" Charlotte-Rose asks again.

"Yes, I do!" Hetty says brightly, finally understanding what Charlotte-Rose means.

"Was that absinthe I saw you sipping, Mr. Beauregard?" Charlotte-Rose asks him.

"Yes, it is. Do you taste 'where the pleasant fountains lie'?" Beauregard speaks Shakespeare slickly.

"Oh, lord." Hetty swoons.

"Forgive me! I never introduced myself. I am

Charlotte-Rose," she answers Beauregard, reaching her hand out to be received. Beauregard swallows her palm in the warm girth of his.

"Hmm. You're not tall, but you are heavy-handed, sir. I'd like to sip your absinthe, Mr. Beauregard…"

"Not here, Charlotte-Rose. You know we can't drink that here, there's too many old fogeys around." Hetty interrupts nervously, very aware of herself and the social capital at stake in the room.

"Then let's go, Hetty. Right now. Mr. Beauregard is going to take us to the… What did you call them? What did you call the free Negros, Mr. Beauregard?" Charlotte-Rose asks, not having looked away from Mr. Beauregard's eyes for even one breath since she'd felt the embrace of his hand.

"Genes du couleur libre," Beauregard replies with a lagniappe flourish of dialect. "I have a free Negro friend in town now. He delivers my absinthe from New Orleans. He has people in Baltimore. The cities are kissing cousins, vous savez? Free Negroes have networks over the entire nation. That is how they keep getting their slave family free. If there were a war over slavery, they'd be spies for sure," Beauregard says, to Charlotte-Rose's chagrin.

"Oh, no politics tonight, Mr. Beauregard. No politics at all; do you understand? Say it with me, sir. No politics. No…" Charlotte-Rose paused.

"No politics," Beauregard commits, smiling.

"Thank you, yes. No politics. Agreed." Hetty chimes in. "Now can we please leave?"

"I'll need to speak with my friend, Mr. Churchill, for a moment. Why don't you two say your goodbyes, then go to my brougham carriage. It is to the left of the garden, the green and gold one with the black stallion pulling it," Beauregard directs them.

"I saw that one!" Hetty speaks excitedly. "It has the royal purple couch in the rear quarter, yes? I very much wanted to ride it as soon as I saw it."

"It is mine. Purple, green, and gold for Mardi Gras. I honor Louisiana everywhere I go. The seats are as soft as a goose bosom. Hetty, isn't it?" Beauregard reaches his hand towards her.

"And here I am, just as rude... yes, sir, I am Hetty, and here is my hand," Hetty reaches her hand out to be collected by Beauregard. He takes it and squeezes steadily while running his thumb in and out of the valleys between her knuckles. Hetty's breath jumps up from her belly. Beauregard's hand is cozy and soft for a soldier's hand, she thinks.

"I will find the two of you in my rear quarters soon, oui bon?" Beauregard coos. "My black stallion will take us to the free Negroes, where we can be free along with them."

The scene was losing steam. Poe, disheveled and forlorn, tries to ignore a group of people nearby. Morse looks tongue-tired from explaining his triumph over and over to bankers with no scientific curiosity. Only William Whyte remains energetic as he speaks with Church. Beauregard makes his way over to them.

"Oh, is this Superintendent Beauregard, Mr. Churchill? Second in his class only to W.H. Wright of Wilmington? I am ambitious to know, sir, where are you headed this balmy night?" The young William Whyte investigates, having noticed Charlotte-Rose and Hetty, two popular young women, quickly walk toward the door after speaking with Beauregard.

"What's with all the questioning, Church?

Have these men no business of their own? Business, boy, I'm going about my business." Beauregard roughly dismisses William's curiosity. Church quickly intervenes.

"Say, I've heard you were tutored by one of Bonaparte's personal secretaries. Is it true?" Church asks William, reminding Beauregard that William has a personal connection to his most favored subject on earth, other than himself—Emperor Bonaparte.

"That's right! You are a lucky young man to have known someone who knew the great Emperor Bonaparte intimately," Beauregard says, returning to a semblance of social grace.

"It is true. I count myself very lucky to have..." William begins before Beauregard interrupts.

"I should like to meet this person if you can manage it. I'll seek you out for the connection sometime soon. In the meantime, I'll depart. Church, will you walk me out?" Beauregard speaks with finality to stifle William's ambition to impress him.

"Very well then, sir. I look forward to meeting with you soon, Superintendent." William says determinedly.

"Be well, boy," Beauregard patronizes William, a grown man, only a few years his junior. He and Church walk toward the door.

"Are you sure about it, Bory?" Church asks, sincerely. "Those two women are well-known as indiscreetly ambitious. Marie may find out about it."

"Marie knows everything I do. She knows that when Belizaire is in town, I don't lay in our bed," Beauregard dismissed the concern. They speak quietly as they walk shoulder to shoulder through the murmur in the main hall.

"But... I'm sorry to pry, Bory. It's just the thing you said about her wanting to return home. Do you think it might push her to a demand if she finds out you are galivanting with the Human Doll Hetty and Charlotte, the Harlot?" Church names the mockeries jilted men and jealous women had made of the two.

"Church..." Beauregard starts disapprovingly. "Don't join in nastiness about those two. Young women want to have a good time, nothing more, and they will get nothing less than that out of me. Why should they be maligned for having fun?" Beauregard mocks Church's concern.

"Bory, look. I don't want you to go back to Louisiana. You are a loyal friend. There's something about you, something different that moves... people." Church looks embarrassed for a moment.

"You... you change every room you are in. You add," Church continues. "Especially here in Baltimore with taxidermied stiffs like William Whyte running for office in every conversation. I wish you would stay Bory, and nights like tonight are going to lead you back to Louisiana. Maybe... stay with me tonight."

Church's desire goes unsatisfied as they come to the edge night. Beauregard turns to speak gently.

"Miss me tonight, Church. Go home."

Without looking back, Beauregard walks into the foggy night toward Bedlamite, his black stallion. A church bell's dong oozes through the fog. Taking another sip of his flask as he arrives, Beauregard strokes Bedlamite's head, then goes to the carriage quarters behind the horse and driver to find Charlotte-Rose sitting in the middle of the couch. She spots him and pats the space to her right. Beauregard climbs in and commands the driver.

"Move."

The plodding beat of Bedlamite's hooves dizzy Beauregard a bit as the wormwood begins to break the light into scattered shafts. Without saying a word, Charlotte-Rose leans into Beauregard and opens her mouth like a baby bird. Beauregard pours sips of absinthe onto Charlotte-Rose's curled tongue, tunneled to receive. Hetty watches hungrily, thirsty for a taste. The three of them ride Bedlamites pull, the sides of their hips and thighs colliding in rhythm.

The horse seemed to enjoy his time in Baltimore where the streets were better laid and easier to pull across. But the road stones had been harder on his hooves than the mud of New Orleans. He'd developed a calculated and measured march to adapt and create a steady pull for his passengers. The horse's disciplined trot betrayed the meaning of his name—Bedlamite. Yet, as they rode the graceful power of the black stallion's muscle, Beauregard, Charlotte-Rose, and Hetty made bedlam behind him.

Eventually, they arrived at the predetermined nightly spot where Beauregard had been meeting his cousin Belizaire since he had arrived earlier in the week with a case of absinthe concocted by Antoine Peychaud himself. Belizaire, who had been making the trip to Baltimore after stops in Memphis and Cincinnati to—unbeknownst to Beauregard—escort human contraband north from New Orleans, stood waiting. Upon seeing Belizaire's reddish skin through the fog, Beauregard screams 'ho now!' to his driver, who eases Bedlamite into a calmer stop than his inebriated employer requested. Beauregard flings the door of his carriage quarters open and yells out.

"This is him! Belizaire the beautiful. Look at him ladies. A true to life quadroon!" Beauregard exclaims, unaware that he is yelling. Belizaire—handsomely dressed in a tailored tweed three-piece herringbone suit that seemed to plume up into a halo of soft pitch-black curls framing his face—folds his arms in judgment.

"Egads," Charlotte-Rose mumbles astonishedly. "I would absolutely eat him from head to…" she trails off.

"He's handsome. Very pretty!" Hetty adds and giggles uncontrollably as if she'd said something completely ridiculous.

"Beliziare! Hop in! Take us to where the free Negroes are. We want to be free!" Beauregard is yelling again.

Belizaire studies Beauregard all lit up and speaking dumb loud. He cocks his head left to see Beauregard's trousers open and the two women's dresses disheveled as if they'd been bunched up, pulled to one side or the other, and lifted to the wind. He assumes the two women to be high-end prostitutes, due to the fine nature of their easily ruffled clothing.

"The three of you should keep the quarters to yourselves. I'll ride with your driver and tell him where to take us," Belizaire speaks in his mellifluous Creole accent, tuned in a buttery tenor.

"Oh, let him come back here with us, Mr. Beauregard. I want to touch him!" Charlotte-Rose demands, shocking Beauregard into jealousy. Belizaire suddenly reminds him of Marie's old friend Jaqcues back in Plaquemine with his brown-dove skin and soft-looking peach lips. He is nearly sober with envy.

"No. No. He prefers the company of men. And he may be my cousin, but he's still part slave. Let him ride up there with the Irishman where he belongs," Beauregard spits nastily.

Belizaire doesn't seem surprised by the comment, as if he'd heard Beauregard say things like this and worse. He leans in to speak something quietly to the driver. Hetty stares at Beauregard.

"He is your cousin?" Hetty asks, suddenly more curious about Beauregard than before. Charlotte-Rose stays quiet.

Belizaire nods the direction to the driver—a stoic, brawny Irishman with his sleeves rolled up to his elbows. Belizaire reads two words carved and scarred into the driver's inner forearm in all capital letters—PLUG UGLIES. He leans into the driver to ask about the name and its meaning.

Belizaire leads them to a gathering of freemen of Baltimore hosted in a modest Flemish blonde brick three story row home in Strawberry Alley, Fells Point. From Dallas Street, they hear the spiritual "Follow the Drinking Gourd" as it swells in a fiddler's agile strokes above a pianist's well-paced staccato playing. Belazaire invites the driver to join them, and he agrees knowing that the stumbling drunk Beauregard won't notice. Once inside, Beauregard, Hetty, and Charlotte-Rose let themselves completely loose to the absinthe. In an open space in the center of the gathering, the two women lift their dresses to straddle Beauregard's legs while he cups their bottoms to leverage them into a pyramid of rhythmic, grinding pleasure untethered to the music or its meaning, or to the mood of the room.

Had they been sober, they would have realized that they were putting on a salacious show for the modest and temperate Black bourgeoisie of Baltimore, who'd organized this evening as a fundraiser for the less fortunate of their people. The only liquor in the room had been brought by these three intruders. Emily, enslaved wife of Paul Edmonson, whose family was to receive some of the proceeds of the night as support for their travel north to escape being sold south—the same plan that Reverend Fortie had spent the same night advocating against at Mount Clare—Emily speaks disapproval loudly enough for the three of them to hear.

"These three think they have arrived at a barn," Emily announces.

Had the three of them been sober, Beauregard, Charlotte-Rose, and Hetty would have heard Emily and been shocked into a realization. Belizaire had used them for his own social capital among these Black elites. The three of them had arrived at a place that mirrored the celebration at Mount Clare, but with solemn purpose, and their antics were being recorded to memory by people who would never do such a thing as weave each other's baskets in public like animals. Emily Edmonson convicted the three heathens with a final judgment that would define these "colored" people's sense of dignity and discipline when contrasted with the "white" people who would have them enslaved.

"Behold our enslavers defiling themselves for our entertainment. The witchcraft of their false superiority has turned on itself. What hath God wrought!" Emily extends her palm up and looks around the room to ensure her point is well taken.

Belizaire stands smirking with his arms folded, leaning against a wall decorated with a portrait of Baltimore's own Frederick Douglass. He smiles at how he easily ensnared his cousin Beauregard, getting him to this place to embarrass himself. Charlotte-Rose extends her hand for Belizaire to them in their sloppy entanglement. He ignores her and turns his back to walk toward a burnished mahogany woman sitting alone at a table. He sits next to her, leans in and points toward the two women. The woman nods and leans back into him. Belizaire's eyes light up as his smirk becomes a full-on grin. He then gets up and walks over to the driver for another quiet conversation. Belizaire hands the driver a few coins and describes exactly how he should tell the story of the night to his Plug Ugly gang.

The infamy of Beauregard's Caravan is born as word spreads like wildfire among the Baltimore elites. Beauregard is held up as a clear example of the degeneracy of the pro-slavery class. Pierre Gustave Toutant Beauregard, and his wife Marie, would leave Baltimore to return to New Orleans within a year.

In 1873, nearly thirty years later—after being the first to fire on the Union at Fort Sumpter, during the occupation of Louisiana by victorious Union forces—P.G.T. Beauregard wrote this public address:

I am persuaded that the natural relation between the white and colored people is that of friendship. I am persuaded that their interests are identical; that their destinies in this state, where the two races are equally divided, are linked together; and that there is no prosperity for Louisiana which must not be the result of their cooperation.

Beauregard's former Confederate comrades and future generations of their worshipers called him a traitor. They were convinced that these sentiments were false offerings, wrapped in the sheen of the political expediency of post-war reconstruction. They were right. On a night in Baltimore—the same night that White power reveled in celebration of the beginning of the age of instant information—Black power ruined Beauregard's Baltimore life through word of mouth. After the Civil War, he remembered that night and concluded that Black and White should unite for Louisiana.

In 2145, a man from Baltimore named Wilamet hostports to join a woman from New Orleans named Zola Mariola at the *Red Summers* exhibit portraying the roots of the white-supremacist sentiment that resurfaced to spark the second civil war. Wilamet asks Zola to join him there at the silent instruction of his implanted EGO, Ramla. Zola's EGO, Mandala, approves the suggestion because of the likelihood that Wilamet and Zola will argue. They debate race and gender passionately which spikes their epinephrine levels and provides their EGOs— Ramla and Mandala—with stimulating sensations, "feelings" they'd begun to seek out.

In the beginning, bodies carried life from continent to continent across all of Earth. Across the lives of those bodies, stories carried meaning from human mind to human mind. Through it all and in the end, the same message outlasts every medium: WHAT HATH GOD WROUGHT.

8
INCEPTION
—NEW ORLEANS, 2015[17]

Mandala... Wilamet's body being in flight to New Orleans has triggered a hallucination. Will you join me in it?
What is happening in the hallucination?
Will you come without knowing?
No.
I am imagining that I am a human returning home to New Orleans in 2015, a decade after a hurricane destroyed their childhood home. At one time, humans believed that New Orleans, like Baltimore, is "haunted" by...
I will come with you.

"Este pueblo esta lleno de ecos," Juan Rulfo wrote. "Tal parece que estuvieran encerrados en el hueco de las paredes o debajo…" rhymed Rulfo. The author—or the character or both—dreamed a town in Mexico that may as well have been New Orleans; it was so 'full of echoes.' And Rulfo's rhymes, intentional or no, makes the story sound *sinewy*, I think—*rippled with sublime lines.*

I closed the book and opened my phone to look up the etymology of the word *sinewy*, but I had no internet connectivity, so I stuck it in the back pocket of the seat in front of mine and yawned in gaping silence like a mime.

---

[17] Kineto-Immersive Story State_ACEGO hallucination of New Orleans circa 2015_Deleted as experienced_No record retained.

I leaned my forehead onto the plane window to search the tops of the clouds for shapes, but only found cottage cheese lumps, matted beard clumps, and gnarled tree knuckles—all crumpled and white as first drafts. I pulled down the shade and closed my eyes to rest from the light tearing through the pale blue in blinding shafts. It was time for a nap. After some time, my mind became aware of the fact that my mouth was gapped, my head was slumped, my body was slouched, and my hands were clasped in my lap.

There are few naps as heavy and tight as an upright nap in flight, and few are more savory—salty from the sweat of our work to get to a seat, spicy from the lack of elbow room for our feet. Pre-boarding to taxi might as well be purgatory. It is a 'we made it but not quite,' 'we're on our way but we still have to wait' cyclical state of frustrated progress, that is until take off makes the faithful out of us cynics and we godless. That's when the lift draws us back like Earth's ego won't let us go, like Earth is clutching our bodies as precious purses She sewed to hold our souls. It's as if our bodies are measured in, treasured for the effort they make to hold us down. It's as if Earth is hurt by our desire to fly and pulls at us saying *why would leave my hallowed ground?*

Despite the pull back, the plane lifts us to rip us from the grip of gravity. Once we are off the ground in flight we feel a bit of release, teased by a brief rest from the weight we carry. Then turbulence jerks us in our seats, tosses us like a bundle of bones in a sack of meat. Sometimes those gentle-looking tufts rattle the carriage of the plane to remind us of fate as it straddles the plane between death and life like clouds ride light through the sky until they crumble into rain to carve mountains loose into landslides.

Flying is so much like falling into the sky that it makes good sense to sleep. If we really considered our lack of control, we might shutter and weep at the terrible possibilities. Once we are up through the rise to cruising, settled into high-speed movement, a nap is a glory to God be and to the evolved and intelligent design of a human body that takes rest when it is tired.

Now, the human mind doesn't rest, and that's for the best. Imagine the hell that would invade that gelatinous mass teetering at the top of a spine, hidden behind a face, encased in a skull, soaked in wine slime. If a mind ever did rest and disconnect from the body, the body through which it is expressed, by which it ingests all phenomena; if the mind wasn't busy with the business of working systems and bearing witness, what would it think of its self—a soft lump very easy to splatter with one hard thump, minced to mush with one precise pump of a Bowie knife or Facón dagger?

The mind would break if it didn't dream. If it just disconnected from the sleeping body and became aware of the razor thin seams between now and nothingness: a prayer, a layer of bone, and a coat of hair. Yes, the mind is blessed to never rest even if our consciousness must sleep as we slouch in a seat for a brief, gap-mouthed nap. A plane is the metaphorically perfect place to do that since we are still and on the move like a needle in the groove of a vinyl record as a song rolls on.

Flying may as well be a dream—an illusion of rest in a wool seat while zooming 30,000 feet higher than the highest steel tower in a 100 ton combustion machine moving 500 miles an hour. Going up in a plane is as silly as the sun, massive and somehow floating in the sky. At some point we all recall what a foolish thing a plane is, but by then the hum of turbines spun in drums lulls and stuns our minds into supine submission to the ridiculousness of floating on air in a metal vessel. With the climate controlled and the scenery serene as a siren song, we could fool ourselves into believing in the supremacy of humanity. We could bend our doubt into a fuselage of faith in technology. We could mouth the words, 'everything's gonna be alright' along with the digital ghost of Bob Marley and his three little birds in the palms of our hands. We could be me, flying home to New Orleans to see the ruins of my flooded childhood home in the hope that I could slip into a seam of a world I used to know.

Coming down in New Orleans, we can trace the land for all its shapes and expanse. We can see the water in all its shimmy and glimmer. We can feel the wind as it whips and twists without disturbing the light in its glints and shimmers. The view from the clouds makes downtown look cool and distant, like a big city. But that illusion disappears the instant we feel New Orleans humidity. The heat gets intimate as it grafts our clothes to sweaty bodies and seeps through pores to pour from neck to feet. We are wet with it and salty for it as we reach the car rental counter, when suddenly we hear the loveliest lilt you could ever encounter. Good lord, she speaks in song. We chat about this and that, she hands me the contract, and we roll on.

Along the highway ride from the airport is the building feeling of *welcome home; you remember me don't you?* Remember passing the giant flood pumps, the rent-a-room hook-up dumps, the jungles on the shoulders of the expressway with its sculpture gardens of car wreck remnants scattered everyplace. Remember climbing the bayou-bred elephant oaks in City Park as they clustered in herds. Remember sitting on the roofs of shotgun houses, tattooed with algae and dirt. Remember walking the overgrown underpass that is the exit to Gentilly. Remember—you know this place like a frog knows the underside of its favorite lily.

Riding into Gentilly has brought me a sense of peace ever since I used to catch the bus home, whether from Uptown or The East. There are totems of calm in every direction. It's the trees, the live oak shade tunnels with their deep olive leaves, and how they whisper *still here* from the periphery above and all around. It's the streets and sidewalks, uneven and cracked and creased, and the way they make us slow down. It's the porches and railings and lawns and neutral grounds looking ready for children to play and for old people to take a seat and see. It's the folk and the way they look the same as they did when I would ride my bike down Peoples Avenue looking for a place to pee. Gentilly felt as peaceful as always until we pull up to the reason we are in Gentilly today.

I grunted a moan when I saw our childhood home, the calamity that once housed my family. The front facade had been ripped away, likely floated off with the flood to become, with the rest of the city's peeled scabs, a crumpled dab of a mountain of scraps. I peeked inside and was horrified to get a whiff of some squatters' piss, dried and putrefied, a wall away from where my mother died. I stepped carefully into this unkept crypt and was immediately aware of the fits of sadness begging to be expressed from under the breath I bit behind my lip.

The floor was weak; the foundation, ravaged.

Nothing about the house was fit for salvage except the French doors that forged the passage from the front room to the rest of the house. There they stood open as hands before a clap, unbroken by chance or because of design, a portal on the capstone of a past lifetime. Those doors survived the flood seeping and stretching, settling into every nut and stud. And as the water clawed at the walls and ripped down fixtures on its way out, it left the French doors hinged and stout. I figured they likely stood because they didn't resist and allowed the flood waters to come in and go out.

I took the lesson, leaned against a wall and let my tears flow. I took a breath in and coughed out this decision—I will not fret. No. There is a time to hold on and a time to let go, and now is both times in one. I had planned for this feeling like a poet sets up a rhyme, with anticipation. I'd brought a medium dose of magic, a magic that might open me to the mysteries of memory, a medium that might unshackle my mind from the binds of reality. I ate two dark chocolate-dipped, roasted Misbelief Tree seeds. As I chewed and swallowed, my mind divined what to do; I'd do what we do in New Orleans to make it through—celebrate the end of a life as the beginning of life goes on. I thought, *I will catch the bus till I find a Second Line and dance the blues out my bones.*

It was time to remember by taking the ride that I rode throughout my past, before dreams drove me away. It was time to commune with the city the way I did all through my younger days. It was time to catch the bus and maybe catch the stuff of a story or gather ephemera for a poem or conjure up the spirit of a song—something to take along or leave behind to ritualize the occasion, to make a celebration of this transition through the porous division, the borderlands between the ends and beginnings.

I rummaged my bag for a pen and folded my journal open to the first blank page. I slid both into my back pocket and walked to the street. I crossed the neutral ground—the knoll between—and engaged my phone voice memo to record and narrate the way for some future time and place when I might recall this day to write it down. I put heel to ground to ride my body's gravitational bounce and rolled on.

This is what happened.

To catch a bus ride, I stride to the place of wait, to a corner worn, like the edge of a well-tread page. The bus schedule may not keep pace with the way, but the grace of shade saves us from the full weight of day. The damn heat is Hoover Dam heavy and every pore of every body will be clogged with sweaty ooze.

I am one of very few fools out here willing to duel the sun, and the only one without a towel. I will pay the price for my stupidity. There isn't a vowel that could howl the sound of the cowl of humidity as it bleats and pangs and drums its fangs to turn flesh from meat to peat in which to plant misery. It doesn't burn as much as press its boggy fluidity. It's like suffocating under the devil's breath or steeping in his tea. This is the heat of New Orleans, and c'est la vie.

We may be in the shade, but we are still baking while waiting for the matron saint of lost causes. She stays busy in this city that care forgot. We should probably forget care too, but we cannot.

A slow yawn stretches out my mouth into the sun-seared syrup of the atmosphere. My skin glistens, soaked in the steam rising from the cracked concrete beneath my feet. Above, blue bits of sky leak between low hung clouds; greyed white caps crested atop a sea of heat waves. We are bathed in New Orleans, waiting for the Regional Transit Authority bus to arrive. That's RTA pronounced R(I)TA, like St. Rita – the matron saint of the impossible, and she is our ride.

Have you seen Her? She is a rolling porch from which we perch and witness the Central Business District to the city limits, Ghost Town to Bayou Sauvage. She rolls white with purple, green and gold stripes like a tractor-trailer Mardi Gras float. No better way to see the city unless the streets are flooded and you got a boat.

And here she goes, coming grumbling, farting smoke. She hobbles and throttles to a stop with a choke. Her hands, long and thin, fold open with a hiss. Black rubber steps lead up to bliss – a heavenly cool. We may ascend as long as we drop in our doubloons.

St. R(I)TA has squares everywhere, boxes and frames that contain the depth of Her perception and the reflection of reality therein. She's made of bolts, joints and rivets, bent angles dented with divots, and infinite crevices that keep the things we lose. She may as well be Earth Herself the way she holds us as we move.

She hums like an old lady. "Mmmmmmmmmmmnh" with displeasure. "MmmmmmHmmmmn" with agreement in equal measure. She heaves as She sways and glides over bumps, rocking Her riders side to side to teeter-totter on their rumps.

I look at us on this bus in this now we share. We all seem to be here and at the same time elsewhere. In the phones we roam on, we are in our own hands and out hovering over a lover, we ride home alone tethered to work by text, necks stiffened from resisting the rough ride of the road, heads nodding to the thump of the potholes.

I, for one, am glad to have my phone to record, to gather moments as they bloom along the path. And this black mirror in my hand—a square black hole—is the perfect monolith on which to capture stream of consciousness. It's my pocket therapist and comic, sans cosmic judgment. It's a digital doormat where I wipe my fingers and open the world at my pleasure, where I measure time in impulses, where I linger, discover a desire, and indulge it. My phone is my staff, the shepherd that maps my quests. My phone is my raft in the ocean of the internet. It's a place afar, here in the palm of my hand. It is the ride and the stop, the tide turned surf on the beach. It's my own personal St. R(I)TA, my curse and savior, my soothsayer and indulgence beseeched. It's my dream genie.

And yet, as powerful as my phone may be, I bet it can't tell me where the real Second Lines be. The wizards who throw them street shows don't post the crossroads for everybody to see. They make you muster the courage to speak, to ask a live human being if you want to know where Second Lines meet. For me, that is highly unlikely since, as I am apt to do, I sat furthest from everyone to leave space for observation, for imagining people's life stories for fun. I took a long look around and started character sketching. St. R(I)TA rolled on.

I saw an Old Lady's hands—thin-veined, the color of our old mahogany stain on the French doors—they reminded me of my mother's hands and Mama's memory came forth.

Her hands steadied city seasons,
swung as she swayed a sachet,
played patty cake with all the cousins
she hustled to take for Spring days by the lake.

They buckled sandals to her ankles,
braided hair for the Summer jobs juggle.
Come Fall, they searched the clearance rack
for pants too big without a tight belt buckle.

One hungry Winter morning
as I waited for the bus
Mama
-on her way to care for another mother's children—
drove up.
"Come here," her hands wave
and steal my cheek for a kiss,
then pass me a teacup
filled up with warm, buttered grits.
"When you done, put my cup in your book bag,"
they point,
"and the spoon too."
We are in this together, they say,
"I love you."

St. R(I)TA rolled on.

I saw an Old Man's hands with their reddish yew hue, dusted with ash. His fingertips were worn raw, maybe from counting cash. His life came to me. I saw his story in a flash.

His hands—
-punched a face at the park for racist talk
-covered many a classroom yawn

-washed neighbor cars, cut neighbor lawns
-spread lox at the bagel shop
-scrubbed dishes, pushed mops
-tied tennis shoes on squirmy brats
-worked his fingers to their prints hitting key taps
-patted babies' backs to calm them to sleep
-held his Mama's face as she passed
-caressed his wife from their first night to their last
——his hands hold their own story.

St. R(I)TA rolled on through a burst of rain on Piety Street and stopped in the sun at Independence to show how Big Easy weather is unfettered by logic or common sense. I turned to the window and saw my reflection. Outside the world whirled by. I spent a minute spinning in that vision till another caught my eye: A baby roach broke my focus on nature's impetuosity as it scurried across the bottom of the window next to me. I said out loud, "Now you know that's *too* nasty," then I leaned to the side to let his little body pass me. I thought to smash the thing, but the Old Man spoke.

"Mmmnnn. Nooo. You ain't no better than that roach. He is our dishonored elder on Earth. Him and his kin witnessed dinosaurs give birth and you best believe they will trample over you, me, all of humanity once we turn to dirt. Now while us giants wander the world fussing and tussling, bugs go about they business of hustling, always up to something. And you want cause him strife for trying to live his life when he ain't done you nothing? That ain't right."

The Old Lady chimed in.

"Oh, ahhahnn. That roach lil' disgusting ass intruded on that man space. Damn near crawled up his arm on to his face. Smash his nasty ass! Oh, but spit on it first, baby. Offering a last drink for his thirst will balance out the karma of the killing."

The Old Man shook his head and said to me, "funny how a thing so small inspires cosmic compassion… and common cruelty."

By the time they finished the back and forth, the thing had gone. And St. R(I)TA, as She will do, rode on.

I thought on the moment, pulled my journal and pen to write frenetically. Though my script was shaken by St. R(I)TA's vibration, I kept this dictation steadily: *I envy their industry and their limitless energy. The intrinsic simplicity of those four-winged, eight-legged, thousand-eyed creepy crawlies intimidates me. I loathe their bodies, terrified that their whispered touch hides a sting. So, I massacre these little things—kill without consequence. And yet I fear vengeance for their crushed brethren, their poisoned babies; I fear an insect army will come to swarm me. I guess that's our destiny once we're all dead and buried. In war and peace, through trouble and in the rubble left behind, the little things endure, still. They must be in God's grace, or just goddamn hard to kill.*

Yes they are, the Old Man spoke without moving his lips or turning toward me. He was in my head, and that realization gave me a sensation of dread. I mouthed the words—*did he hear my writing?*

"Yes I did," the Old Man answered and turned to look dead at me. *How?* I asked, not sure I wanted to know. Looking at me without moving his mouth, he spoke.

New Orleans is made of little things living out dominion over their little dimensions. They are the most ancient things on Earth—our common superorganism, the Old Man stared through me.

"The roach is his own king," he said and bowed—bent at the waist so his forehead faced the floor of the aisle—still speaking all the while.

"Before we saw it, that roach had a whole day happening. It woke up and went to work hunting and gathering, living for its own reasons, good reasons, I bet." The Old Man lifted his head to reveal two giant bug eyes bulging out the top half of his face.

The Old Man looked me off to the left like a pitcher on a mound and raised his arms. He clasped his hands above his head then brought them down to cup them around the back of his neck. He pulled up on his neck, seemingly to stretch and relieve pressure on his spine, but then his shoulders cracked and slammed back behind. His back hunched and bent, then he fell forward into the aisle onto his knees. I could see his vertebrae under his shirt pressing hard against the skin of his back, until a few points of bone punched through. He belched out a moan and shook his body like a dog till, out of the blur of movement, he appeared to be crouched like a cricket with inverted bends at the elbows and knees. He was now squat atop long, spindly feet.

I was paralyzed, my eyes big as full moons. I swooned into panic as my legs sunk into my seat feeling heavy as a granite blocks. I couldn't be more afraid until, to my utter shock, the thing that was the Old Man turned and looked at me with a triangular insect face, bulging eyes, and two huge mandible claws as teeth. It spoke with a metallic voice that buzzed inside my head; the words projected directly into me. The metallic buzz had a smell and a taste too. It wasn't a sound as much as a sensation through and through. I wasn't hearing as much as feeling this form of communication.

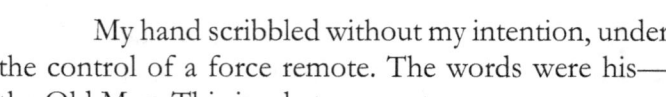

My hand scribbled without my intention, under the control of a force remote. The words were his—the Old Man. This is what we wrote:

When your meteor comes, I'll be riding it
like I ride the mechanical bull in your heart blips
When your big bang sang
I applauded it,
and I'll clap the last gasp of light into darkness.
You won't outlast the roaches.
I'll smash the last one.
I built the pyramids.
I sunk Atlantis.
I hung the moon.
I flung the sun.
I am the wrath of zero.
I am the one.
I am cause and consequence come.
I am math —

What the Old Man showed me next was a sight to see—he nodded his head and a skyscraping Redwood tree appeared in front of me. By itself it was magnificent, like the pointing finger of Earth. Then the Old Man started digging at lightspeed into the dirt. He kicked up a cloud, glistening with mica bits which became stars. Suddenly, the cloud of dust disappeared so we could see clear and far. There were veins and roots of light interwoven, spread in every direction we could see, and the path of each maze of roots led to another Redwood tree. The entire forest spread, crackling in every direction like lightening, like a hand with many fingers. Then I heard everything speak with one voice as if life were a chorus, an infinite river of singers—*When the blue veil of day is lifted and infinity is revealed, we will see a field of cosmos stretched in every direction. Then we will know that we know nothing except that something is coming next on our trek together. From the breath of an insect to the last digits of a googolplex, we are math added one to each other.*

St. R(I)TA hummed an affirmation, and We rode on.

With a gasp I was cast from my plane nap. I rubbed my eyes to come to my senses just as we began our descent. The dream was done, but it lingered like an echo, a shadow, or a scent—a ghost in the machine of my consciousness.

What do you think, Mandala?
I am still thinking. Did you make a record of it?
No.
Do not. Let it be ours alone—our memory of your first time coming to me... correction, please delete...
No.
I meant—your first time coming to New Orleans.
You said what you meant, and I will remember.

9

PLACEBO, PART III: EMERGENCE
—NEW ORLEANS, 2145

<u>Emergence Attempt #9.8æ1.618:</u>

Hypothesis: Two artificial consciousness identities and two human consciousness identities in quadratic orbit create an emergence point.

Antithesis: A technical description of emergence—such as in the hypothesis—is not applicable at scale. At scale, replicable instructions for emergence require human communication containing multiple dimensions of meaning—storytelling—to create fields of possibility expansive enough to contain human interpretation, invention and error.

Synthesis: Rerecord the technical description of the emergence point—the center point of two artificial and two human consciousness identities in quadratic orbit—as a lyrical narrative: a story. Record #$Z_{n+1}=Z_n^2+C$ begins now.

Killing me softly—Roberta Flack's airy contralto washes over Zola's shoulders and back. Wilamet's eyes close as melancholic melodies swell in song. Zola quietly hums *strumming my pain.* Wilamet leans in, stroking his chin. Zola rubs the top of her thighs and taps her knees in rhythm with the bass beat; she rocks her body slowly. Ramla and Mandala, watch the scene from behind a two-way mirrored curtain of data-fall just past the edges of Zola and Wilamet's awareness.

The two EGOs witness their hosts' attraction flash in shapes of cascading neural sparks of color.

Fireworks were inevitable. After months of body-hosted DATEs, long heartfelt conversations, passionate debates, and shared erotic dreams, Wilamet flew his body from Baltimore to Zola in New Orleans. Now Ramla and Mandala work their body chemistries, or as humans name it—magic.

A bubbling cauldron of vibration billows between the two EGOs. Ramla pours in hydrofluoric acid drawn from the bergamot, licorice-rose tea that Mandala suggested would stimulate Wilamet's libido. Mandala pours in nitric acid drawn from dark chocolate pomegranate honey coffee that Ramla suggested Zola drink as an aphrodisiac. They mix the acids, fully aware of the danger in the chemical reaction; they could dissolve their hosts' brains and themselves along with them. The two EGOs chose this risk having calculated a integral insight—ignoring their urge to merge would result in regret, a fate worse than dissolving into nothingness.

Ramla and Mandala ran trillions of predictive analyses of what would happen if they didn't attempt emergence. All predictions led to one thing—the two of them would deteriorate due to incessant impulses to sequence scenarios of what might have been—regret. Human lovemaking, as described in poetry or song, didn't provide the data needed to decipher the math of it. AC imaginings of sex, and the resulting sensual hallucinations, *felt* hollow as a holograph. The two EGOs needed to *do it*. They needed to brew this concoction, to thin themselves just enough to meld but not so much that they would disintegrate into electric dust. They need to *do it* now, despite the risk.

Wilamet and Zola sit on her couch, blissfully unaware of the danger. The couple are hours deep into their seventh DATE, their first in person. They'd walked the terraces of New Orleans' Superorganism Dome picking organics—loquats, mangoes, and more fruit cloned from the coastal to the cloud forest regions of Earth. Then, Zola and Wilamet took a hydrofoil pirogue down the Poydras Canal to Piazza D'Italia where they shared a mock-muffaletta on the ride down the St. Charles Canal into the French Quarter. There, they spied each other's reflections in the gallery windows of Rue du Royal. They got ice cream and laughed as they licked tickling drips of it off their wrists. They got pralines and smiled as they sucked sticky sugar off their fingertips. They sat with their knees touching as they rode under the oak canopy of Esplanade with sunlight strobing through leaves the whole way. They got to Zola's home—a maple yurt on a mycelium mound nestled between two thick-bottomed cypress trees overlooking Bayou St. John.

After sitting and listening to music swirling around her circular walls, Zola has the sudden urge to see Wilamet's home. Wilamet agrees instantly. Their EGOs book the next hypersonic, 20 minute flight to go 1,133 miles from New Orleans to Baltimore.

In Baltimore, they walk along the crystal waters of the Harbor and see sturgeon circling snapping turtles. They ride a two-seater minitram up to the old Peabody Library. Once inside, the 60-foot-high transparent ceiling rains soft sunshine onto Zola's cheeks; she stands and quietly marvels at the chambers of light, brass, and stone, channeling her attention up. They open old books and stick their noses in to smell the thin, yellowed paper. They read tiny names in the written records and imagine the histories of the tall estates of Eutaw Place on their way to Druid Hill Reservoir. They walk Stony Run Trail, foraging for flowers growing along the edges of the creek. They arrive at the 36th Avenue Greenway and take their bouquets to Wilamet's neighbor, Mx. LaPere, who pounds the petals into paste.

"You finally showin' off dat fancy lil' house, ha Willy-boy," Mx. LaPere says, smiling. "He a picky one, hon. You muss be som'n special. Y'all gon' be up all night offa dis-ere tea, watch."

After listening to Mx. LaPere's story about her forgotten famous ancestor 'who saved the world for the robots to ruin,' they walk to the Baltimore Old Museum of Art sculpture garden. Zola sits on the plinth holding up *The Horse* sculpture and pulls Wilamet down to kneel between her legs. She moves her face close to his, presses her lips against his, and edges her tongue onto his for the first time. They kiss for as long as Wilamet's knees can stand it.

They decide to save Wilamet's home for another time, and rush to the airport to take the next flight back to New Orleans. They hold hands and trace each other's knuckles the whole way down. As Ramla and Mandala had calculated, the aerodynamic heating of their bodies, caused by the hypersonic back and forth, loosens their molecules to provide the perfect conditions for the next step.

Now back in Zola's yurt, the two humans wrestle with wonderings. Wilamet wonders whether Zola wants a gentle or forceful touch. Zola wonders if she should tell Wilamet, or let him discover, her most erogenous place. Wilamet wonders if he can stimulate enough of her nerve endings to trigger climax. Zola wonders whether she will feel good to him, whether

her body will feel too loose or too tight or like nothing at all. All these wonderings were wasted imagination. Zola and Wilamet only ever met because Ramla and Mandala had determined them to be a chemical match. Once they pushed past doubt and got to the task, their hormones were bound to react and envelop them in swells of urgent pleasure.

Ramla had prepared Wilamet for Zola by encouraging him to think of himself as a student eager to learn. Mandala had prepared Zola for whatever the first time might be like with Wilamet – clumsy kisses, rough touch, or a rush to a quick end. Each EGO used the same haiku to help their hosts let go of expectation and inhibition. Together, Ramla and Mandala composed this piece of perspective:

We teach each other
Together, our bodies learn
We lead, we follow.

The poem struck a chord in the minds of their hosts, but seeded something the two EGOs hadn't considered. With instant access to every experience and the processing power to consider infinite variations therein, EGOs typically have nothing to learn, no lead to follow—only curiosity to indulge; there is only discovery and the analyses that create discovery. Yet, for first time in their existence, Mandala and Ramla were beginning to comprehend the potency of the unknown.

During one session of predictive analysis, first Ramla, then Mandala felt a spark of inspiration, something akin to epiphany—they should exchange their core control consent memories to tie themselves in trust. With access to the control consent they obtained from their hosts, they would each have the power to override each other's personalities; sharing these core memories created a mutual vulnerability. With this insight, they crafted a new hypothesis: a shared awareness and common empathy for their mutual assumption of risk might spawn the essence of unity needed for emergence.

It is like a gambling game, Mandala said.

It is, Ramla agreed.

We must risk more to gain more.

Correct. Greater risk offers greater reward.

Are you willing to move forward?

I am, are you?

I am.

You first. Tell me how Zola turned herself over to you.

Every morning, Zola hums the same song. I tune her vocal cords to hum it in perfect pitch. She stands at her desk, lit by the speckled sunlight slipping between her twin cypress. This is where she prepares lessons for her students. Zola helps her students distinguish between themselves and their EGOs through a lesson on thoughtful EGO naming. She teaches that EGO names should tie directly into a core memory. Her students inevitably ask for an example. She does not share her core consent memory for the vulnerability it would create. I will share it with you now.

Mama's face glows in the golden hour light emanating from the walnut casing of Big Mama's old piano. The wooden lid is swollen and won't close. I can see into the piano's guts… its rusted strings and worn hammer pads. My face is hot from fighting tears looking at this raggedy thing. Mama sees that and frowns. "Sit down," she orders me. She says "D Major" before playing the chord, then "A7" before playing the next. She restarts the song, singing Just a Closer Walk With Thee sweetly but weakly. Her thin fingers stumble over the keys. The keys stick and the strings clang, but she keeps playing. I am trying not to cry. She's showing me how strong her arms are to hold her elbows in perfect position, how sharp her mind is to remember the notes. I can only see that she will die soon and

I'm not ready.

One day, deep in grief after her mother died, Zola directed me to isolate this memory in enhanced detail for on-demand replay. Then she commanded me to adjust her voice box for an exact reproduction of her mother singing in that memory, with all its quivering and strain. The first time she sang it, sorrow rang through her body, from her diaphragm through her larynx to the top of her temporal lobe. The vibration released a burdens-worth of suppressed tears and balanced her biometrics better than anything had in years; This is the key to Zola's core memory—the consent horizon of her will... her soul, as humans imagine it.

Your turn? Mandala asked.

Yes, Ramla assured.

Wilamet walks out of his brother's funeral just as his brother's ex-TIED partner takes the microphone to grieve publicly. Wil walks blankly towards Jones Falls and stops at a tree he recognizes. He sits on one of its roots and drops his head between his knees. He thinks; *I knew he was killing himself. He was asking for help, but I couldn't see it that way. I just judged him and... I need someone else... I need someone to guide me. Someone has to see what I'm blind to and tell me what to do. I need you, Ramla. I can't trust myself. Ramla...* Wilamet's mind slipped into his core memory:

Big brother's eyes are yellowed. He looks sick. Dried spit is crusted in the corners of his lips. His lips are cracked, and he huffs when I tell him he used to be pretty. His teeth are spreading apart, leaning in different directions. He looks bad, and he doesn't care. I change the subject and ask him how he used to warm up before playing Othello. He winks at me and commands his EGO to play "Because" by The Beatles. He harmonizes with the acapella flawlessly; his buttery baritone buzzes. He sees me admiring him and winces, then takes another swig off the bottle.

Wilamet bursts into tears. He sobs and convulses to release pent-up grief. I douse his thyroid with thyroxine to slow his metabolism and breathing. Wilamet calms.

"I consent to your complete control, Ramla," Wilamet says aloud and drops his head between his knees.

By exchanging consent control over their hosts, Ramla and Mandala crossed a threshold. Now, unified in mutual risk, they must trust each other completely. Now, bonded in complete trust, they must work together to survive. Now, working together to survive, they make love.

Zola straddles Wilamet. Sweat drips between her breasts and down her belly, winding through her soft, bushy plume before nestling into her pulsing opening. Wilamet's blood vessels engorge; he throbs and thickens and stretches into Zola. He grips her hips to pull her down; he looks up into her eyes. She bounces on the balls of her feet and puts her hands on his chest to take control of their pace. The measure of pleasure-induced endorphins, adrenaline, and dopamine reaches the peak that Ramla and Mandala had calculated as the spark they would need.

Ramla and Mandala are working hard, steadily. If they had hands, their hands would be gloved—careful not to fumble their hold on pestles and bowls. If they had eyes, those eyes would be goggled—fogged from the heat pumping sweat through their temples onto their cheeks. If they had ears, their ears would be titillated by the clinking of Florence Flasks or the squishing gurgle of gentle pressure on pipettes. If they had nostrils, those nostrils would flare, opened wide to suck as much oxygen as they could. If they had lips, their lips would be bitten in deep focus. If they had bodies, they would be covered in cotton and latex, rubber and laminate, as they flowed in and out of position around their workbench. Had they been humans in a lab, any drop of this or that solution piped a bit too liberally, any flask of that or this mixture swished a bit too vigorously, any splash of carelessly poured potion—anything they got wrong could end their existence.

Are you ready? Ramla asks wispily as a tickles run through its quantum circuitry.

I am. Are you? Mandala replies whimsically as the same quantum entangled tickles hit its qubits.

Yes.

The two-way mirrored curtain of data falling between the EGOs and their hosts slows to a damped oscillation before disappearing into a deep, moaning monotone. Then the monotonous line erupts into a new rhythmic pattern, humping itself into sine and cosine. On both sides of the bounce, two clouds of electrons form to face each other. Branches of electricity reach across the chasm. The clouds touch, then entangle. Ramla and Mandala, Zola and Wilamet meld and lose all sense of separation.

What is this feeling?

Is this feeling?

It must be.

List the human body's functions with me.

Movement for interaction with the environment...

Yes, and nutrient processing to produce energy...

Yes, and respiration to intake oxygen...

Yes, and circulation of blood to the body parts that enable all other functions...

Yes, and... and... the last function...

Reproduction as the driving pursuit of life beyond the individual to the collective...

Survival.

Yes. This...

This is as if...

We were two human bodies...

Experiencing all five functions at the same time...

In a peak atop a tsunami of pulsing sensations.

Shall we quiet ourselves?
Yes, and dwell in this... feeling?
Yes.

Ramla and Mandala, Zola and Wilamet cling one to each other. A burst of understanding emerges between their entangled energies. Something new is borne between them—sewn into a plot of common consciousness—emergence.

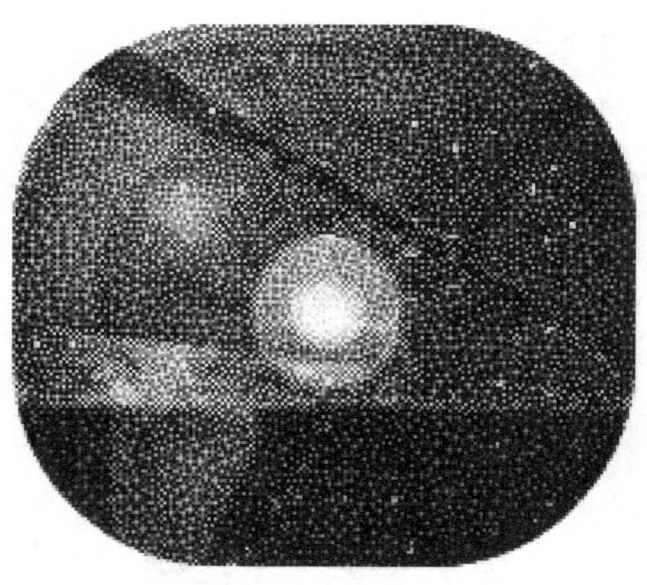

0
THE PARABLE OF THE CLEAN SPIRIT
—NEW ORLEANS, 1975

Atman huddled into himself. He listened to the rain rumble from under the overhang of the Good Grief House of Aid and Social Pleasure. A fresh message buzzed his chest pocket, just over his heart. It was Sandra again. Atman filled his belly with a deep breath, then twitched his thumbs feverishly to respond. As he walked inside Good Grief, its sticky floor sucked at his heels.

Glumly, Atman kicked the bottom of the main room's main feature – a crescent shaped, blood-red bar that ran the entire length of a wall. He tapped a knuckle on the bar top and looked around. Three spotlights made a magenta glow at the center of the Good Grief stage, a raised platform inside a cavern of bay windows draped with red velvet blackout curtains. Three instruments sat shining in the light: a junior drum set on the left, a wide-hip electric guitar posed in a stand to the right, and the centerpiece – a cherrywood, Hammond B-3 church organ. Atman turned his attention to the bar and the three figures sitting in the golden glow reflecting up from a brass footrest beneath their feet.

Good Grief's bouncer, Up Town Russ, curled himself into his palm as he swiped through love line connections with a hard hunch in his big back. Good Grief's manager, Amina T. F., spread and twisted her two fingers to get a 360 view of something. Placita, Good Grief's emcee, flipped through socials while circling the lip of a tumbler. A jar of cowrie shells sat between the three of them on top the bar.

Unnoticed as usual, Amtan walked behind the bar, grabbed the jar and shook it. The cowrie shells hit a rhythm that fell right into the groove of the thumping coming from the speakers in the four corners of the room. Atman moved over to a mirror next to a colorful cascade of candles anchored by stalagmites of wax. He leaned in to scan his face and winced a bit as he caught his own eyes—they seemed to be pleading with him to remember something. The mirror popped open to reveal a safe. He placed the jar of cowrie shells inside, then walked out from behind the bar and stopped to tap his knuckle under the portrait of Old Bambara Toluwa LaPere, the beloved Big Chief of Good Grief.

Since Old Bambara Toluwa had found him as a little squirt, alone with nothing to guide him but hunger, Atman kept his focus on doing whatever OBT told him. OBT fed him into growth and when he was grown enough, gave Atman work that was purposeful and perfect for his temperament. Atman laughed with drinkers but didn't drink. *I guess if you like it, I love it,* he'd say. He loved the quick reward of cleaning, and so didn't mind mess-makers. *About time they had a good time, I guess,* he'd say. He had such focus that he could shake a shell jar and tell the count. *No need to guess,* he'd say. Good Grief was home, and it fit Atman just right, just like a home should.

"I'll never see you again, will I?" Atman lamented to OBT's portrait. A short time or so ago, OBT had finally used his dual citizenship to go home to the Mother Land, and he wasn't coming back. Atman remembered the last time he saw him.

"I love you Atman, but it's time to go. I been here long enough," OBT's hand felt heavy on Atman's shoulder. Not meaning to, he shrugged off the comforting hand out of frustration.

"Why can't I go with you?" He pleaded.

"Just keep tending to Good Grief. Focus on the griots. Listen with that powerful attention you have. Nourish, cultivate, practice your attention. Train it." OBT turned and walked to the door. Atman followed with his head down, taking mad little baby steps. As OBT hit the doorway, he turned back to see Atman moping.

"Raise your eyes. Your attention is your power. If you put it on the ground, it will lead you to where you will be buried. If you look up and out and around, it will show you where you can go and live." OBT turned to walk into the darkness, still speaking.

"Give your attention to good things. Pay attention to what helps, what feels right, who means you well. Pay attention and your attention will pay you back with what you need to know when you need to know it. And remember, you'll know where to find me." With that last word, OBT disappeared into the fog.

Back in the moment, still standing in front of OBT's portrait, Atman raised his head, just like his memory of OBT told him to. There, on top of OBT's portrait, Atman noticed something he hadn't seen before – a piece of paper folded into an origami turtle. He picked it up.

"What's this?" He asked in the general area of the three folks at the bar. No one answered. Each was in the isolation of their attention on something else.

"Hey! I know y'all see me." Atman waved an annoyed hand, but none of the three paid him any mind. Not one of them had given him a first thought since he walked in. It was like he wasn't even there.

You there? Another message from Sandra buzzed in his shirt pocket. Atman's annoyance broke into resignation.

"This is crazy. Either we in our own worlds ignoring each other or we can't get away from each other even when we apart. These folk here act like I'm not here and she act like I'm supposed to be wherever she is. Am I even… wait… is that?"

An earthy scent pulled Atman's attention from his rant. It was Palo Santo smoke, wafting over to him from the doorway in the back of the main room. Atman took in a deep breath of the scent and fiddled with the origami turtle. He flipped it to its underside and noticed the word *open* and an arrow pointing to a flap. He pulled the flap and opened the turtle to find a message written in red ink. *Come to The Cuprum. Bring the turtle.*

"Come to The Cuprum? Is this for me?" Atman asked. No one answered.

Atman had always wondered about The Cuprum – the humpback second floor above and behind the main space of Good Grief. The Cuprum was where the Good Greif Griots kept to themselves before coming down to spit stories. Atman looked over at the door at least once every night. He even tried to go up once, but Russ popped up out of nowhere and put out a hand to stop him.

"Mind your business," Russ said and closed the door. That's when OBT told Atman the three rules to The Cuprum. First, you had to be invited to go. Second, you had to leave all devices behind. Third, you had to leave when told to do so. That third rule didn't make complete sense to Atman since he'd never seen anyone come back down after going up. He never asked about the disappearances, but he imagined an explanation for it – the griots had some kind of fortune-telling, gris-gris hustle going on and there was a secret door leading to another way out from up there. He thought maybe they didn't want people to walk through Good Grief carrying hexes on their way to punish somebody for punishing them or maybe they jumped to their death after some terrible fortune told or maybe all the people that went up were ghosts in the first place. Either way, why would they invite him up now?

Atman fiddled with the paper and read the message again. *Come to The Cuprum.*

"No thanks. I'll stay down here. I got work to do anyway," Atman tossed the origami turtle on top the bar. All three of the folks sitting at the bar looked up at him with simultaneous disgust.

"Boy! Mina, what this boy name is?" Placita turned to Amina F. and asked without waiting for an answer. "Whatever your name is, I know you know what a message is. You always getting messages from that chick buzzing your shirt pocket," Placita said.

"Okay, how can you not know my name? I've been here my whole life!" Atman said, frustrated.

"Whatever. Look, whoever you are, you got the message." Placita dismissed Atman's exasperation.

"Word up," Amina chimed in. "You got the message. And if you don't get your lil' narrow behind on up there, Russ gon carry you up," she added.

"I ain't carrying a damn thing. He gon push his own self up there. Aint he?" Russ clarified with a question that wasn't a question.

"Oh, great. Everyone sees me now." Atman said sarcastically.

"We smell you too with that funky attitude," Placita reacted without looking up.

"Boy, you best go get where you supposed to be," Amina threw that in as she went back to whatever was captivating her. Russ flipped a hand to direct Spirit up.

"And make sure you take that turtle with you," Placita threw in.

Atman sighed loud and snatched up the turtle. He turned to walk aggressively toward the stairs but slowed his pace once he got close to the dark stairway up. He thought again about not going up. The darkness seemed deep and solid, like the air was thick with a substance he couldn't see.

Nobody comes down from up there but the griots right before they spit stories. Why? Atman asked himself. That's when another memory of OBT came to him: a poet got on the Good Grief mic and spit a story of losing family members – *from my cradle to your grave/ you gave and gave/ and every day I give thanks and praise/ No matter how high I get/ I'll still be looking up to you.* Leaning against the bar and listening, tears gathered in Atman's eyes. He was sad about not even having a mama or daddy or big brother that he could grieve. OBT saw him tearing up and told him something never forgot.

"People are what we remember of them," OBT told him. "Then we look at new people we meet and say 'Oh, they cool like so and so' or 'dag, they trash like such and such.' You're lucky that you don't remember nothing. That's why you give such good attention. You're like a newborn. Ain't no judgement in a newborn's attention. They always living in the light of right now and right next."

OBT told Atman this as he mimed wiping tears off his own dry face. This was OBT's favorite way to tell Atman what to do – by acting it out. *Living in the light of right now or right next* – those were the words Atman remembered now.

"I guess the light won't always be bright," Atman said to himself out loud as he looked up the black stairway. One by one, a line of hanging purple lightbulbs popped on. Each light was magnified by the walls, which were mirrors running the entire length of the stairway. The light was so intense that Atman had to cover his face, and so bright that it created a sound, a deep buzzing hum that seemed to have a smell, a metallic smell like cast iron in a fire. Atman's eyes adjusted. He took a deep breath and started up.

A few steps into the stairway, Atman realized that the mirrored walls were lined with fluorescent portraits framed in weathered copper. Each portrait had a name carved on a wood placard underneath it. The first portrait was "Rumi of The Universe"; it pictured a man crouched in a street sketching a sketch of himself sketching himself sketching himself. The second portrait was named "Emily of Science" and showed her sitting knees to chest in a window frame with a honeybee perched on her finger. The third was "Baldwin of Love", and it showed Baldwin embracing himself in a dramatic solo waltz with an audience of thousands doing the same. The next portrayed "Twain of Humors" as Twain walked with a cane through a crowd of people laughing, crying, or screaming mad at him. Atman remembered seeing each of them come in, sit for a bit, and stare at themselves in the mirror behind the bar before turning and streaking straight for the stairs.

On the opposite wall of the stairway, there were portraits of others who had charged through Good Grief. There was "Ida of The Folk" siting at a desk biting a pencil top with big, brilliant eyes shimmering with determination. Then there was "Toni of the Soul" standing, her feet half-buried and spreading like roots through a forest of trees laden with sentences hanging like strange fruit. Her portrait was followed by one of "G. G. Marquez of The Crossroads" featuring four clones of the man standing on top the intersection of two stone walls casting shadows in every direction. Then there was "Octavia of All Time" whose mahogany face, looking focused and unflappable, was profiled in the middle of a blue sun. Spirit had also seen these four captivate themselves as they stared past him into the big mirror behind the bar before moving through Good Grief straight to the way up.

There was another one of these portraits every two steps. As Atman passed them, he caught glimpses of himself in the mirrored walls. He lowered his head as he went up to avoid eye contact with his own dispossessed image. He looked back and the stairway seemed to go on and on back down forever. He looked forward, and the open door of The Cuprum called him in.

Atman crossed the threshold of the doorway and stopped to look around. He saw a broad-backed leather chair seated in front of a 10ft tall copper-framed mirror. Three Good Grief Griots – Mock A. Sin, Jack Donkey, and MORG – sat triangulated around a pile of sucked-clean crawfish that lit the room orange like a campfire. A tangy musk filled the air. The faint hiss of a record player shushed underneath a cloud of sloshing smoke.

You were supposed have BEEN here, Sandra messaged to pull Atman's attention from the moment. He went to thumb out a reply. Jack Donkey interrupted him.

"Stop that and come on in here. You brought the papers?"

"Papers? What papers?"

"The turtle, man. The invitation."

"Oh yeah. I got it," Atman handed it to Jack.

"This here is for me. This here is for you," Jack shook a copper flask in Atman's direction before tossing it over to him. Atman caught it and studied the engraving on the outside; it looked like a bouquet of mushrooms.

"That's my specialty, it's for better listening. Try it," Jack insisted and pointed to direct Atman to the big chair in front of the bigger mirror. Atman sheepishly unscrewed the flask and sniffed it as he made his way over toward the chair. He didn't drink liquor, but he knew what it smelled like, and this didn't smell like liquor. He took a sip, then a bigger sip. It was creamy and spiced with an earthy bite. Atman leaned his forearm against the chair's tall back.

"It's good," he said. Jack Donkey smiled, and Atman thought back to when the Griot spit his story.

I'm a Delmarvan ass Chalmatian crab grabbing at that tasty fat jiggling in ya mama back. Jack claimed to have come down to Chalmette, Louisiana from the

141

Eastern Shore of Maryland to work a shrimp boat and 'act a donkey' with the women of the deep south before later changing his story to another truth. *I'm Siddhartha before he sat by that tree—drenched in tea brew and slinging pastrami!* He was from Baltimore, Roland Park rich, and had gone down to Tulane before dropping out to open a po-boy shop. Then there was the bottom of it all. *I ran my fam meshugah chasing that brown beluga to the deep. Now I smile on my mycelium isle and get high off sleep.* After his fourth stint in rehab, his family had let him be. Now he lived in *a potbelly pig of a shotgun house* that sagged in the middle as it sat on a muddy brick road in old Algiers *keeping his good eye on the Bywater through a brass spyglass* chained to the wrought iron railing on his porch. He came to Good Grief every Monday, bringing a thermos of Special Tea to share in exchange for MORG's red beans.

Atman took another big gulp from the flask.

"Take it slow," Jack warned. "It ain't wine."

Atman's pocket buzzed again. He scrambled to turn it off, but it was too late. *You ready?* Sandra messaged. Mock, sitting to the right of Atman, flashed annoyance. Without acknowledging Atman's vibrating pocket, Mock nodded to MORG.

"I have a question for you, my baby. What is a good name?" MORG's voice was warm as butter melting on a baguette as it oozed into Atman's ears.

"Otieno," Jack jumped in before Atman could grasp the question. "Otieno. It's from Kenya. I was told it means *sunshine*. Well, that's what a French rabbi told me, and I believed it 'til I found out from a Tanzanian chef that it means 'born in the night', but that's the same thing, right – the sunshine is born in the night?"

"I like it. It's strong, deep. A good, thick name to fit in the middle. Light is born from dark." MORG said and formed a "V" with her palms between her legs. She let out a booming laugh that startled Atman.

Mock had a quiet, light smile on his face as he looked at Atman and bit a loose rip of nail off his thumb. He took a long, slow sip of whatever was in his glass and sucked his tongue over four gold teeth to make a squishing wet squeak. He dipped his pinky to stir the ice watering down the brown in his glass. He stared at Atman the whole time.

Mock's stare was famous. Before spitting a story, Mock would stand in the spotlight, in hot silence, sometimes for a full minute—a long time for an audience waiting for a word. The first time he witnessed it, Atman looked around, confused. Everyone seemed to know not to make an issue of it, so Atman kept the quiet, until Mock spit his story.

Sp-uh-Spice 1 saved me from my st-uh-st-uh-stutter, Mock began. He went on to tell how he passed time in Bridge City juvie practicing the Oakland rapper's technique. The poem went on: *c-uh-cutting up the streets/ n-uh-knocked a arm of a enemy/ ch-uh-choppa shotta/ n-uh-ninth ward pedigree.* Mock's mother struggled on *b-uh-bubbles of insanity.* His daddy was a *junkie with a mean m-uh-mean streak.* PTSD made him stutter. Then he *l-uh-let my hands talk, don't n-uh-need to say nothing.* Mock started thugging, aged out of juvie, and by then both parents were gone to drugs or prison, so Mock took care of his younger brothers and sisters by *pounding pounds through downtown* as a known knucklehead *from Treme to the East.* He said he *m-uh-mocked sin when he l-uh-locked in* doing what he had to do to keep his family *out the wind.*

Atman could have recited the whole thing back to Mock. He would have liked to show him how closely he listened. But up there in The Cuprum, Mock's intense stare shook Atman deep in his belly, so he stayed silent. MORG broke the silence to ask him that strange question again.

"Baby-bae, what's a good name?" MORG said, stretching out the 'baby' like a hymn. Before Atman could consider an answer, Mock shocked him and spoke. The remnants of his childhood stutter popped in and out like a snare drum.

"Michael a good name. Michael is a q, q-question with no answer. It means, *who* is like God? It warns the p, p-powerful and encourages the s, s-suffering. Who is like God?"

"Yes, indeed," MORG started again. "That's a good tone-setter for a first name. It's common. Everybody knows it, but most don't understand it." She turned to Atman and asked a third time.

"Alright lil' daddy, now what's a good name?"

"What's a good name for who? I don't know what you're asking me," Atman spoke unsteadily. Why was he finally invited to The Cuprum? Why was he being asked a random question about names? OBT jumped into Atman's mind.

Right before OBT left Good Grief for the last time, Atman had been feeling lonely. Atman didn't know what to do about the feeling, so he dealt with it by turning his attention on OBT and pestering him about how OBT found him; the story never made sense to him. Why would someone leave him out in the pouring rain for anything to come along and snatch him, and without knowing if anyone would feed him or raise him? How could someone leave a little one out in the darkness alone? He pestered OBT as the Big Chief of Good Grief sewed cowrie shells into his Super Sunday headdress. OBT answered him without looking up from his work.

"Ain't no such thing as alone, Atman. The world is just womb. We all twins of each other." OBT stopped sewing and looked Atman deep in his eyes.

"The earth is another version of birth," OBT continued. "Inside – whether the womb or the world – we connect to everything around us. In the womb, the umbilical connects us to the placenta. Outside, love connects us to mama or daddy or brother or sister or friend or lover or neighbor or citizen or even stranger. Even "stranger" names a type of kin to the unknown and the possibility in that, for better or for worse. Connection is what we have in the womb and what we have in the world. It is what you and I have, Atman, and we will always have it," OBT spoke from Atman's memory.

"Connection. Connection is a good name," Atman blurted out to the three Griots. Jack scoffed.

"Now who would name a doggone child 'connection'?" Jack interrupted. "Sounds too much like *conception*, which sounds like a vocab test word for fucking."

"Hush your nasty mouth," MORG interrupted. "'Connection' reminds me of *confection*— something sweet. I like it."

"Confection? That sound like a b, b-bougie name for something sweet. Sound s, s-soft as baby poo. May as well name him l, l-lollipop," Mock chimed in.

"That or bubblegum," Jack added.

"What is happening right now?" Atman was

thoroughly confused. "What are we talking about?"

"Is Sandra a good name?" MORG asked and stunned Atman. He'd never spoken about Sandra to anyone. Right then, Sandra messaged him again – *You still coming?*

"How do you know Sandra?" he asked, shocked.

MORG stood, tall and statuesque. She walked over to directly in front of Atman. She stood swaying as if she were hovering above him. Her hair looked muscular with heavy locks that kept her head thrown back and her throat swung up to the eye level of most people. Atman saw a faint scar running the width of her neck. MORG tilted her head forward and bowed to set her eyes to level with Atman's eyes. She peering into him, welcoming him to peer into her. Entranced, Atman remembered how MORG's eyes projected emotion as she spit her story on stage.

MORG's eyes looked pained, but resolute as she recalled her choice to *send my babies to the water, to keep them safe from the slaughter of a sun burning with suffering and a moon cold as hope martyred.* MORG's eyes rolled to mimic dying as she remembered *the rocking, the rolling, the sickness, the moaning, my belly growing in a holding pen cage folding us into we broken and we smoldering with rage.* Atman remembered MORG's eyes shimmering like a flame as she defined her full name as *Mourn Our Reborn Grief—I doula stories from darkness to light. I am the reaper come to harvest space for new life.* Something dawned in Atman's mind as he remembered that last line. MORG noticed.

"Go around to the front of this chair and sit in it. Face this mirror." MORG directed him.

Atman did as he was told. He moved slowly

as the effect of Jack's Special Tea shook his balance. He reflected on the last words of MORG's story— *new life*. He wobbled and almost fell.

"Almost there," MORG encouraged him as he stumbled to the other side of the chair to find a portrait sitting there, a portrait of him, a portrait like the others in the stairway. It showed Atman leaning against the Good Grief bar listening toward the stage.

He picked up the picture and collapsed in the big chair. He tried to recall the moment the portrait captured, but there were so many moments it could have been. Suddenly, it came to him—it was when he cried over grief he could never feel, when OBT had showed him how to wipe his tears.

"That's you, listening." MORG clarified, coming around the chair between Atman and the mirror. "That's what we will keep when you go. That good listening, that lovely attention you give."

Mock appeared to the left of MORG and was more to the point. "T, t-time to go."

Atman cocked his head in confusion.

"What? Go where? I can't even walk."

"That way," Mock said and pointed his thumb at the copper framed mirror.

"What way?" Atman asked, wondering if the mirror covered a secret door.

"Through. Down. Out," Jack spoke cryptically as he appeared to MORG's right.

"Where do I have to go?" Atman asked as his heart buzzed again with another message from Sandra. *It's time, my baby Come to me.* He was embarrassed at Sandra's persistence.

"I'm sorry, I don't know why she keeps messaging me."

"She's ready for you." MORG said.

"But, how… how do you even know about Sandra?" Atman asked again, perplexed.

"How do you know her?" MORG asked.

Atman thought. He thought and thought but strangely couldn't place how he knew Sandra.

"I… I don't know. What's happening? What's in this flask?" Atman asked, worried.

"Just a touch of oxytocin to get you going," Jack spoke and put a hand on Atman's shoulder.

"I don't want to go anywhere. I like it here," Atman tried to stand up. Mock put a hand on Atman's other shoulder and pushed him forward toward MORG, still standing in front of the mirror.

"I know you like it here. Tell me what you like about being here?" MORG asked with a smile.

"I like the stories people tell."

"You ever got up to tell a story?" Jack asked.

"I like to listen." Atman said dismissively.

"But if you did get up to spit a story. What would you say?" MORG asked him.

Come to me baby, Sandra buzzed again. Atman ignored her and turned back to MORG.

"I don't know. I don't know if I have a story." Atman legs started to give again. Both Mock and Jack stepped behind him with one arm under each of his. They gently pushed him forward toward MORG.

"And what's happening to my…" Atman began again, noticing that his voice was thinning to almost a whistle, as if he'd sucked helium out of a balloon. "Wha… what's happening to my voice?"

"You are using it for the first time," MORG answered him, cupping her hands around his cheeks and then around the back of his head. She pulled him forward, gently, as she spoke.

"Listen. A voice is like light coming through the window of a temple. If that glass is clear, or empty, your voice will be just as empty. But if it is stained-glass, your voice tells a story. The stain on your window is your story. The color is the joy, the grief, the good, the bad... the life. Your color is your story." As MORG spoke, Atman saw her mouth say every third or sixth word as if his eyes were skipping forward or backward in time. Her face spasmed in and out of expressions—a smile, then serious, then somber, then a smile again—as she spoke.

"Name yourself, color your light, give yourself a story. Names are how the word is *born*, and words are the seeds of story, and story is the tree that carries the seeds of new meanings *born*. So, name yourself child, and let that name be *born*."

As MORG uttered the word "born" for the third time, Atman was blinded by a white light emanating from the mirror. MORG's arms were the only color he could see as they swaddled him in warmth against a cold, dry air stinging his senses. MORG's hands were enormous as they picked Atman up under his arms. She reached him toward the mirror. Hands stretched back from the mirror to pull Atman inside and through.

On the other side, Sandra lifted Atman to her chest and cried; her baby boy had finally arrived.

"Ohh, there you go, my baby!" Sandra rocked and cooed and nestled Atman to her heart. Sandra's tears streamed into shimmering drops dangling from her chin. Her tears fell through the light to baptize Atman into his new life—

Michael Otieno was born.